Renee,

ONE WEEKEND IN LOS ANGELES

AUBREY BONDURANT

This is a work of fiction. Names, characters, businesses, places, events and incidents are either the products of the author's imagination or used in a fictitious manner. Any resemblance to actual persons, living or dead, or actual events is purely coincidental.
This book is for mature audiences only.
Cover Design by Kim Wilson of KiWi Cover Design Co.
Text copyright © 2024 by Aubrey Bondurant
ISBN-13 : 979-8884129054

PROLOGUE

Andrea

"Babe, you have to do this. Please," my husband, Jeff, beseeched, sitting beside me on our hand-me-down sofa. We were in the one-bedroom apartment we'd rented last year when we'd moved to Los Angeles so he could pursue his music and acting dreams.

I took a deep breath before trying to explain my concerns. "I'm anxious about putting our lives out there for the world to see. Think about what the publicity could do to our relationship."

We'd been together since high school, and I was secure in our commitment, but appearing on a reality show seemed like going under a microscope where the world could dissect every little thing. I had my doubts as to how healthy it would be for us.

He stood up and paced, running a hand through his blond hair before coming over and dropping to his knees in front of me. "I promise this won't change things for us. We're as solid as they come, babe. Consider what this could do for my band or for my shot at future acting gigs. *City of Angels* is the big break. I can feel it deep in my bones."

He took my hands between his, and I was hard-pressed to say no. His band had been his dream since high school, and acting had been his passion. We'd always been each other's biggest supporters. "I worry."

He kissed my hands. "I understand, but I swear to you, I will always be the man you married. And if it becomes too much, I will choose you over the show and leave the minute you say so. Scratch that—the second you say so."

How could I say no to his earnest face? The thing about Jeff I'd always admired was his honesty. If he said he'd walk away, then I trusted he would walk. "Okay. Let's do it."

His handsome face broke into a boyish smile, the same one I'd fallen for eight years ago in our junior year of high school when he'd asked me to be his lab partner in chemistry. I'd trusted in him when he wanted to leave our small town and go away to college and when he wanted to move to LA. This would be no different. I'd trust him. I'd trust in our relationship. And I'd trust we'd be just fine.

Chapter One
ANDREA

"What are you going to do?" My PR rep, Ollie, asked me this gently while sitting across from me on the ridiculously expensive sofa which wasn't at all comfortable but Jeff had wanted because he'd seen it in a music video. Ollie had been good enough to come over this morning, bearing fruit and bagels.

"We'll do what all the other reality couples do. Get divorced." My tone was flat and void of emotion despite the deep wound of betrayal lodged in my chest.

He put his hand over mine, sympathy reflected in his weathered face. "You should consider making a public statement."

Right. Because it wasn't enough to have my husband cheat on me, but the news of his infidelity had been splashed all over the Internet and picked up by the tabloids. My world had been rocked after finding out he'd cheated with our twenty-two-year-old co-star in an alley after his last concert.

"Can I disappear and never say a word?" I loved how supportive most people had been since the video had gone viral, but there were others online who used any excuse to be nasty. They were the crowd dissecting my relationship like armchair therapists.

"You could disappear, but it would mean it's only his narrative out there for the world, only his version of reality."

Fucking reality. For two years my reality had been cameras documenting our lives while Jeff's mediocre band played small venues around the country and pretended to be rock stars. He'd lapped up every second of newfound fame, accepted product endorsements by the dozen, and clamored for every acting crumb passed his way.

It seemed as though we'd done more public appearances with cameras in our faces than spent actual time together over the last twenty-four months. And after he'd invested in a new bar two months ago, he'd put in many late nights there. The perfect cover for a cheater.

City of Angels had taken off on the Drago network after the first season. We'd gotten to the point where Jeff and I had bought a million-dollar home, drove the types of cars that required high-grade gasoline, and I'd been told by the producers to trade in my Target wardrobe for name brands. In two seasons we'd become grade C+ reality star celebrities.

He'd promised he wouldn't change from the midwestern boy next door who'd captured my heart at sixteen, but over the last two years, we both had. And it hadn't been for the better.

I'd come to resent the cameras in my face and always having to be on, while he'd been so desperate for the attention he'd often called the paparazzi to tell them where we'd be. The most intrusive part had been the photogs stalking my stomach over the past six months, apparently hoping I'd announce a pregnancy. This was especially heartbreaking since I would've given anything for it to be true.

At the beginning of this last filming season, I'd been ready to walk away from *City of Angels*. To go back to concentrating on our marriage and starting a family. But Jeff hadn't kept his promise about choosing me over the show. Then again, it wasn't the only promise he'd broken.

"Someday it won't hurt." It was my new affirmation.

"You're right. Someday it won't hurt. If you ask me, it's an early midlife crisis. He's eager for attention, and Paula gave him the ego boost he was seeking, meanwhile she's searching for an identity and will happily take on the one he provides her even if it costs her in the long run."

Jeff's willingness to do absolutely anything for attention wasn't news. As if his cheating wasn't bad enough, he'd done so with someone I'd befriended and defended from the others on the show. I'd considered Paula young, naïve, and sometimes irresponsible, but I'd always seen the good in her. Hell, she'd even spent last Easter with us.

My stomach heaved at the memory. Had they been sleeping together three months ago? I had no timeline. No answers. Partially my own doing. Too blinded by my initial shock and despair, I hadn't asked any of those questions when I'd confronted my husband. He'd admitted to the affair, said he might be in love with her, and told me he'd needed time to figure his head out, whatever that meant. I hadn't seen him since.

We'd have to talk again eventually. We shared a home. Cars. A dog. As if on cue, Callie, our shepherd mix, laid her head on my lap. At least dogs were loyal.

"Any chance you're considering forgiveness?" Ollie didn't say this with judgment but only genuine concern.

"I can't." Even if Jeff begged for forgiveness, I couldn't overlook the way he'd changed. There'd been problems from the beginning of the show and over the last year especially, but this was the last straw. The Jeff I'd known and loved since high school was gone. In his place was this celebrity-status-chasing poser who glued himself to his phone to find out earnings of others and everything we needed to do to keep up with the Joneses.

"Take your time and address your fans when you're ready."

I'd never get used to the idea I had fans. I was a normal person who'd appeared on a show as myself. It wasn't as if I'd displayed any talent or anything. Disappearing sounded better than a statement, but there were genuine people out there who'd been invested in the two seasons, and me, and I wanted them to know how I was doing.

"I'll write an Instagram post tonight." Then probably never log in again.

"Want me to look it over? We have a team—"

I stopped him. "No, it'll be from me. Unfiltered and honest." I was done having a team do anything for me, unless it was my makeup. Boy, did I need an army to help on that front these days. My eyes were puffy and my skin lackluster from not sleeping or eating over the last few days. At least my job had been understanding about my taking time off this week.

"Here's an idea. How about after you make your post, you go out this Saturday looking hot and unbothered? Deacon Miller is playing SoFi Stadium here in LA, and I have an extra ticket."

I chuckled at the irony since Jeff would've given anything to see the legendary rock star in concert. He practically worshipped the guy.

Ollie wiggled his brows. "It would bother your ex to see pics of you there."

Hearing Jeff dubbed my ex sounded foreign. Like I was

living in an alternate universe and any moment things would go back to the way they used to be. But every morning when I woke up, the situation hadn't reverted. How did you go, in a matter of hours, from believing you would spend the rest of your life with someone to knowing it was over? My brain couldn't deal with the whiplash.

My eyes rolled. "Is this the person I've become? Doing petty things to annoy Jeff?"

He put his weathered hand on mine. "No, and that's what makes you special, Andrea. But you do need to kick your ass into gear and show some pride. Not for him, not for the world, but for you. From the first time I met you both, I thought this fucking girl can do better than this self-absorbed wannabe celebrity, and I'd like to see you get out there and smile again. It's killing me to see you this way."

It was killing me too. But as much as I'd have loved to prove to the world I could put on my big-girl panties and carry on, I didn't know how to start.

Unauthorized tears running down my face only underscored my losing battle. I wiped at them angrily. "I'm tired of being pathetic."

"You're not pathetic. You're grieving the loss of a marriage and the life you thought you had."

I inhaled a shaky breath. Not for the first time, it occurred to me that perhaps I'd been grieving the loss of the relationship for a while. Wondering just where in the hell the person I'd fallen in love with had disappeared to. "I do want to control the narrative to my own story." Which meant I needed to take action. Fake it until I could make it. I had three days to get it together in time for the concert. "All right. I'll go."

He leaned back, a smile splitting his face. "Excellent. I'll book a glam squad to get over here on Saturday."

Come Saturday afternoon, the reflection in the mirror surprised me. While on the inside I was numb and barely treading emotional water, the outside said, "I'm hot and ready to party like I'm single."

Never had I worn a skirt this short, let alone one made of leather. My boobs were cinched up in a crop top which showed off abs which were flat thanks to the "my husband cheated on me so I've only drunk wine" diet. My plain brown hair was now highlighted with golden streaks which livened it up. And my makeup was really wow. Dramatic colors I'd never choose for myself painted my lids and played up the emerald-green eyes Jeff used to say were my best feature.

Nope. I refused to think of him. Turning around, I surveyed my ass, which I had to say was looking good, even if it was barely covered by the skirt. "How will I go up stairs?"

Portia, the stylist Ollie had brought over, snorted. "Carefully. You want boy shorts for under? Or, if you ask me, wear nothing."

"Boy shorts, please." Baby steps into what I was deeming my fake rebound phase. Because I might appear as though I was ready to move on, but my heart was far from in it.

Ollie walked in wearing a crushed velvet suit of deep plum only he could pull off. He whistled at my outfit but then, reading my expression, waved a finger in the air. "No, ma'am. Get that look off your face right now. Tonight is Deacon's last show of the tour, and it's going to be epic."

"I'm not sure." Suddenly facing the public seemed like a monumental task.

"Come on. I mentioned you're coming tonight to Deacon."

I tried not to roll my eyes. As if Deacon freaking Miller, bona fide sex symbol, rock star, and notorious bachelor, would give a shit about little old me. "Uh-huh."

Ollie held out his arm. "Time to get out there and show the world what Jeff was stupid enough to lose."

Chapter Two

DEACON

On Friday morning I settled into the luxurious leather back seat of the Cadillac Escalade which had picked me up from the tarmac where my private jet had just landed. I was fighting serious jet lag after my red-eye flight from Boston, but I still had a long day ahead of me now that I was back in LA.

As I dialed my PR agent, I downed a bottle of water and waited for him to pick up.

"Hi, Deacon," Ollie greeted. "How was the flight?"

"All right. Anxious to get some real sleep though."

"I can imagine. After your concert on Saturday, you plan to stay in LA long?"

"Couple of weeks." I owned several properties around the world, including a home here overlooking the city, but there was only one place I could relax completely. My modern, but comfortable, beach house retreat about sixty miles north of Sydney, Australia. It was my oasis.

I'd been on a twenty-two-state US tour over the summer, and played Asia and Europe the year before. Although I loved what I did—the fans, the music, the travel, and performing—I was ready to take a break and have nothing on the schedule. Get back to songwriting and the simple life without having a half dozen people in the room with me at all times.

My sigh must've been audible because Ollie's next words were, "You doing okay, Deacon?"

"Yeah, just tired." Tired not only of the grind, but of the public light. Constant cameras everywhere and people trying to mooch off my success. Recently there was the added drama of my breakup with Nina and her subsequent whirlwind engagement only two months later.

"Have you decided if you'll attend the wedding?"

It didn't bother me to see my ex move on quickly, but having her walk down the aisle with my stepbrother was a nightmare. The goal was to have a clean break from an ex-girlfriend, not have her join my family.

When I'd first been asked to attend their wedding, my response had been an automatic "no fucking way." I'd send them a gift and wish them well from afar.

"Nina told the tabloids you're not over her, and that's why you might not attend."

My eyes rolled. Nina and I had only dated for three months, and it had never been love. At least not on my part. She might maintain she was brokenhearted from the breakup. Considering she'd immediately moved on to my stepbrother, I wasn't convinced she had a heart to break.

Bryce wasn't a bad guy, but he definitely didn't realize what a manipulating drama queen he was marrying. The fact he'd probably taken out a loan to finance the rock on her hand showed how besotted he was with her.

"My mom called yesterday to ask me to please attend." I understood her desire to have the family together and was hard-pressed to tell her no. She was the single mother who'd worked two jobs so I could have music lessons while growing up. My stepfather, Rob, was a decent guy, and in any other circumstance, attending my stepbrother's wedding would've been a given.

"Want my advice?"

"Always." Ollie was good people in an industry that didn't have many, and I trusted him implicitly.

"Go to the wedding and take a date. It'll show the world you're unaffected, and then you can be done. At least until Christmas, when you'll have to figure out if you're going to avoid the family gathering because of your new sister-in-law."

"Fuck." I hadn't thought that far into the future. Would my ex be permanently engrained in my life? If Nina were a sweet girl without an agenda, I could get past the discomfort, but she was more the sort of woman to create all kinds of family drama.

"We could always schedule you a holiday concert series. Say the word."

It wasn't the worst idea, nor would it be the first family holiday I'd missed due to my schedule. "Let's keep that idea in our back pocket." I'd be shocked if Bryce and Nina lasted until a second Christmas. "I'll see you at the concert on Saturday, right?"

"Yes, you will. I have a favor to ask about your concert, actually. One of my other clients, Andrea Foreman from *City of Angels*, recently went through a rough time. She'll be at the concert, and I was thinking you could throw a wink her way or something. Poor girl was cheated on by her husband who's a narcissist wannabe rock star. It would be a nice boon to her confidence."

Hearing anyone have to deal with a narcissist was a trigger for me. After all, I'd grown up with one until my mother had finally gathered the courage to leave him. "Happy to. Where will she be?" I'd toss her a guitar pick and blow her a kiss or something.

"Next to me, left center in the third row back."

"Thought you were taking Roger?" Since they both lived in LA, I'd assumed Ollie's long-term partner would be his plus-one.

"No offense and don't ever tell him I said this to you, but while he adores you personally, my boy, he does not appreciate loud music or crowds."

I had to chuckle. While Ollie was flamboyant and down to party, despite being slightly north of sixty, Roger was conservative and did the lawyerly thing in a suit most days. The kind which wasn't made out of crushed velvet. Guess opposites really could attract. "Fair enough. See you tomorrow night."

"THIRTY MINUTES, DEACON." A rap came at my door with the warning for showtime. My wardrobe person, Pam, handed me my jacket while I warmed up my vocals.

Once I was on stage, the crowd fueled my adrenaline. There was no bigger high than hearing people sing back the words you'd put your heart and soul into. Four songs in, my gaze found Ollie left center, three rows back. And damn, was that the woman he'd mentioned—what was her name—Andrea?

I didn't know what I'd expected, but the brunette was stunning. And it wasn't just the skimpy outfit which showcased her curvy body, but the shy smile she offered up.

Most women I met at concerts had a level of aggression akin to a pit bull with a raw steak in front of them. But she gently swayed with the music, her bright eyes sparkling with the genuine joy of simply experiencing the moment.

My next two songs were electric as I let the sound of the music feed my soul. My voice was on point, my band completely in sync. I loved the way my fingers strummed over the guitar and played the chorus. I knew I was experiencing the high of the sprint to the finish line. Another ninety minutes, and I could celebrate with my band and start a long-overdue vacation.

As I finished my next song, I glanced back toward Ollie, but he was engaged in animated conversation with the woman who was pointing at her phone, tears visible on her pretty face even from up here on stage.

Fuck this. Nobody cried at my concerts. After the end of the song, I shouted over to the stage manager. "I need a spotlight."

"Where you want it, Deacon?"

"Left center, third row. Lady in the blue leather outfit next to the guy in the plum suit."

"On it."

The spotlight caught her off guard, and as the lights went up on me, I stepped closer to the edge of the stage. "Ladies and gentlemen, I have a special guest tonight. Some of you might recognize her."

I nodded to the two security guys in front. "Bring her up, will you?"

She stood there stunned, but then Ollie took her phone and gave her a little push. Gotta say, never had a woman need to be shoved toward me before.

As soon as she came up and was featured on the big screens, the crowd started to get loud. "Any of you know Andrea Foreman from the *City of Angels*?"

The crowd went nuts. Far be it from me to judge reality

television, but the magnitude of my fans' recognition of her took me aback. I wasn't the only one, for her entire face turned red.

As she came closer, I realized she was more beautiful than I'd seen from afar. Not in an enhanced way, but in her natural beauty. For a moment all I could do was stare until I remembered everyone was waiting.

Time to play up the audience. "You know what I heard, Andrea? I heard you've shed some dead weight recently, and are newly single."

The response was deafening. And I even managed to coax a tug of her lips.

"What do you think, Los Angeles? Do you believe I could sweet-talk a kiss from her?"

The crowd lost their fucking minds. Even my band mates, most of whom I'd been with over the last decade, stood there with wide eyes at the unexpected reaction. Now it was time to deliver. The question was whether I had a willing participant. Once again, not something I'd ever had to worry about before now. Flipping off the hot mic, I asked, "Are you okay?"

She let out a long breath. "I thought you were just going to smile at me or something from the stage."

My grin came easily. "Or something. You okay with a kiss on the cheek?" It wasn't my intention to make her uncomfortable, and it would be cute for the crowd.

There was enough hesitation to chip at my ego, but at the same time fueling me with the excitement of an unfamiliar challenge. She gazed out into the stadium, unintentionally playing it up, with the anticipation of the moment taking on a life of its own.

Then she turned, leaned toward me, and pecked my cheek.

Of course I grabbed my heart and played it up as though it was the best thing to ever happen to me.

But the audience wasn't having the cop-out. Like a heartbeat, they started chanting, "Kiss her, kiss her, kiss her."

"I don't think that did it for them. You okay with giving them another kiss on the cheek or really give them what they want?"

"Wouldn't want to disappoint the fans." Her lopsided grin made me do the same.

"No, we wouldn't."

Stepping into her, I framed her face, aware of the way the entire stadium was watching with bated breath. My gaze locked on hers, and I moved to touch my mouth to hers. I'd intended to do a quick brush of the lips, but suddenly my thoughts were gone. The crowd faded into a distant background, and instead all I could focus on was the fullness of her bottom lip as I took it between my teeth. She opened her mouth to gasp, and I took advantage, swiping my tongue inside.

It should've ended there. It was more than enough to satisfy the fans, but not for me. As if a live wire was attached to my spine sending zaps of energy to the tips of my toes, I instantly craved her.

Banding my free arm around her waist, I hauled her closer, now aware how her body was shaking. Or shit, maybe it was mine. Because this kiss had suddenly taken a sharp turn into dangerous territory. The type that had me wanting her to wrap her legs around me and walk her into my dressing room where I would take her against the wall.

But I suddenly remembered where I was and the fact this was intended to be a cute stunt, not a full-on make-out session. Pulling back took a monumental effort, but I forced myself to do so.

Andrea looked as stunned as I felt. Leaning forward for her ear only, I whispered, "Smile for the cameras, beautiful."

My statement did the trick. She snapped back to life, taking an unfortunate step back from me and breaking the spell which had somehow found itself on stage with us.

Regaining my senses, I flipped the mic back on.

"Now that's how a REAL rock star kisses the girl," I quipped. The fans ate up every word of the obvious dig at her wannabe rock-star husband.

Taking Andrea's hand, I brought her knuckles to my lips and kissed it not ready to let her go entirely. Leaning in, I whispered, "Have Ollie bring you backstage after, all right?"

"Um, sure. Thanks."

The hesitation in her reply made me wonder if she'd actually be there.

Chapter Three
ANDREA

One minute I was reading a report on my phone about my ex having his mistress over at our house and arguing with Ollie about leaving the concert to deal with the situation, and the next I was getting escorted on stage to kiss the world's most eligible bachelor.

If only Deacon's kiss hadn't been so incredible. How unfair to measure every future date to a sexy rock star who kissed like, well, a sexy rock star.

But while I'd been stunned, he'd merely been going through the motions. Hell, he probably brought a girl up every concert to run the same schtick. That's why I hadn't bothered to stay for the aftershow. It was time to get back to reality.

It had been a fun escape, I thought, making my way to the waiting Uber. Ollie had beseeched me not to go to the house yet in case Jeff and Paula were still there, but it was in fact my home. My bed. God, the thought made me sick. What if Jeff had slept with Paula in my bed?

Just when I thought I could be strong and move on, the

past threatened to pull me under with some new revelation exposing a new way to spiral into depths of anger.

As I pulled up to my house, I noticed it was dark, and when I came in the front door, the only sound was the alarm beeping at my arrival. Good. Maybe they weren't here.

After walking into the kitchen, I set down my purse with a breath of annoyance. We'd finished decorating the house last month, and now we'd have to sell it. Running my hand over the marble countertop I'd spent weeks picking out, I let the tears fall.

It wasn't fair. Yes, relationships ended. Yes, people were entitled to find their happiness, but my husband had chosen to pursue his while still with me. While I'd been sitting in the doctor's office making an appointment to start our IVF journey next week, he'd lived a double life. The thought made me sick to my stomach, but I wiped my tears and forced myself to avoid the familiar round of useless thoughts. How could I have been so stupid? So blind?

No. This was his fault. And beating myself up for not suspecting my husband of lying and cheating was victim blaming.

After a long shower, I put on my pajamas and curled up in a freshly changed bed. I automatically reached for my phone, frowning at the forty-six notifications and eighteen missed calls, some from Ollie, some from my parents, and the majority from unknown numbers.

The sight triggered me back to the night the news had broken about my husband cheating. A video catching him and Paula in the alley behind a bar making out, and my life had fallen apart.

Taking a deep breath to steady myself, I scrolled to the text from Ollie, which included an attached video clip. I clicked on it and gasped.

The video showed me up on the stage tonight kissing Deacon Miller. Watching the playback was surreal. It was difficult to process the woman up on stage had been me. Then he delivered the line about being kissed by a real rock star, and the crowd went wild.

For the first time in the last few days, a genuine smile crossed my lips.

I dialed Ollie's number and was relieved when he picked up on the first ring.

"You're the talk of the town, darling." His words were difficult to hear against the background noise.

"I'm not sure that's a good thing."

"Are you kidding? You told me you were tired of feeling pathetic. Consider this as the icing on the karma cake you're now eating. By the way, there was a very disappointed Deacon when you didn't come backstage with me tonight."

"Yeah, right." I doubted he realized I was missing from his party. "Is that where you are now?"

"Yeah. And your on-stage kiss is all the buzz."

Was I blushing? Maybe I did deserved this boost even if it was fake. "It was definitely my highlight of the month."

"The press is eating it up."

Something in the media about me aside from the cheating scandal was a nice change of pace. Then I heard the sound of the Ring camera security chirp, indicating someone was at the front door. I stiffened. "Shit. Jeff is here."

Ollie sighed. "Is it too much for him to leave you alone? He puts you through hell and comes and goes with complete disregard to your feelings?"

I'd looked into changing the locks, but I couldn't legally keep him from the property since we were co-owners. But he hadn't stayed here in days, so why now? "Hopefully he'll grab whatever he forgot and leave me alone."

I'd taken up residence in the master bedroom and moved all of his things into the guest room. There was no reason for him to come in here even if he insisted on entering a house where he was definitely not welcome.

But it wasn't to be. He stormed into the master bedroom as if he had every right, holding his phone to flash a picture of me kissing Deacon Miller. "What the fuck is this, Andrea?"

It was on the tip of my tongue to tell him it was a fucking phone, but I managed a shrug instead.

"You really think I'd believe you and Deacon Miller have something going on? You're not in his league, and this won't work to make me jealous. Just a pathetic PR stunt."

He thundered out the same way he'd come, leaving me shaking.

"A narcissist can't stand to be upstaged, and he definitely is jealous. As if I couldn't hate him any more than I already do," Ollie muttered over the phone. "Arsehole."

"Who's the asshole?" came a masculine voice I recognized immediately even over the background noise of the party.

"I'll let you go, Ollie. Enjoy the party." I hung up the phone quickly not wanting either man to hear me cry at the callous way my soon-to-be ex-husband had spoken to me.

My phone immediately buzzed back with Ollie's number. Answering it, emotion clogged my throat. "I'm not in the best mood to talk."

"What will get you in the mood?" came the sinful voice of Deacon Miller.

"A lot more than you can give me over the phone."

I wasn't sure who was more surprised by my words, me or him, for silence hung between us. Then he let out a chuckle. "One more reason why you should be here instead of hanging around assholes."

I noticed the background noise had gone quiet. "Wouldn't be the first time I made the wrong choice."

"Could be the last."

A smile curved my lips. Flirting with Deacon was officially my new favorite thing. "I bet you say that to all the girls."

"If you would've stayed, you would've found out I don't."

Damn if he wasn't good for my fractured ego. "I wouldn't have been good company. I'll let you go so you can have some fun at your wrap party. Thanks for tonight."

"Any time, Andi. Good night."

He'd called me Andi. Something I'd never let anyone call me more than once. It didn't matter considering this was surely the last time I'd ever speak to him.

As for tomorrow, it was time to stop dwelling on the past and take steps to put it behind me. I'd start by meeting with a divorce attorney.

Chapter Four
DEACON

I was intrigued by Andrea Foreman. And I couldn't remember the last time I'd felt that way. An hour after our call, done with celebrating my last concert of the tour, I sat in the back of my large SUV with Ollie, and he gave me the rundown on her soon-to-be ex-husband and the whole situation. Right down to her ex's reaction to my kissing Andrea tonight.

A curse left my lips. "I don't even know him, and I hate him."

Ollie nodded. "Welcome to the masses. Bona fide narcissist who can't help but victim blame and takes no accountability for his shitty actions. Then he has the audacity to lash out at her when he feels jealous as if he hasn't put her through enough."

"What if—?" I stopped myself at my wild idea.

But Ollie perked up. "What if what?"

"Never mind. She doesn't need to be playing games right now."

"No, she doesn't, but at the same time, the concert tonight was a big help in reclaiming her confidence."

I contemplated for a moment before deciding to float my idea. "I was thinking she should join me at the wedding next Friday. It would kill two birds with one stone by showing both our exes we can do much better than them."

Ollie's brows went sky high. "You'd make people believe you're dating?"

"Let them assume what they want." They did that with every woman I so much as talked to. Tabloids didn't care about the truth, just what sold.

Ollie wavered. "You're a good guy, Deacon, but I don't want Andrea getting hurt again."

"I have no intention of leading her on or hurting her, I promise. Even if she was in a position to start a new relationship, I'm off to Australia in a week and not looking to start anything. It would only be for show."

I'd had relationships, but I'd never wanted to settle down with anyone. My lifestyle consisted of traveling around the world on tours and then requiring solitude for weeks at a time while I wrote.

Generally, I preferred my own company to that of others. None of that lent itself to long-term commitment. Kids were something I could see myself wanting in the future, but I wasn't optimistic about finding someone who could cope with my chaotic life and bring the type of balance that would allow for both my music career and a family life.

Ollie appeared thoughtful. "The *City of Angels* wrap party is Saturday night. Andrea is under contract to attend and has been dreading the event since her ex will be there along with his fling, but maybe if you took her…"

"That would work." One weekend. Two nights. Two dates. Two exes who could learn the world did not revolve around them and get the message we were both moving on.

"She'd need to be talked into it."

"I can be very convincing." Yet, somehow, I knew Andrea would be a challenge. The idea made me even more excited to talk with her.

Chapter Five

ANDREA

The smartest decision I'd made during my marriage was to keep my professional career. At least this way I still had my independence and wasn't left without an income going forward. Being a computer programmer who worked from home allowed me to deep dive into work without leaving the house.

It was a darn good thing I didn't have to go anywhere since I had paparazzi camped across the street. While the cheating scandal had garnered a fair amount of attention, kissing Deacon Miller up on stage had catapulted me into tabloid-stalking territory.

It had been tempting to visit home, a small town in Kansas, but since my mom and Jeff's mom held a joint belief that I should forgive him and move past this "phase Jeff is going through," that wasn't the best place for me. It was apparently tough for them to comprehend our breakup was permanent.

So when Ollie suggested a massage appointment on Friday morning, I jumped at the chance for some relaxation. As I sat in his SUV on the way to the massage spa, my muscles practically twitched in anticipation.

"You didn't have to drive me today, Ollie. Gifting me the massage was nice enough." Now that people knew my car, it was better for me not to drive it, but I could've taken an Uber.

"It's on my way to one of my own appointments, so it was no trouble. And there's something I wanted to talk to you about."

"If it's about doing an interview to tell my side of the story, I haven't decided whether to do it yet."

It was bad enough I was contractually obligated to go to the season wrap party on Saturday night, but the producers wanted me to do a sit-down to talk about the affair. I wasn't sure I had it in me. On the other hand, I didn't love the idea of Jeff being the only one telling the story. Not only did he blame me for his inability to be faithful, but he seemed to relish the opportunity.

I'd written a quick Instagram post letting people know I appreciated their support and to please respect my privacy, but it seemed the latter was impossible.

"You should do what makes you feel comfortable when it comes to the interview. But as for the wrap party, I was thinking perhaps you might take a date."

"It's sweet of you to offer to go with me, Ollie, but—"

He chuckled. "No, dear, not me. Deacon Miller."

The mere sound of his name caused butterflies to take flight in my stomach.

Ollie pulled into the parking lot of what appeared to be an urban oasis tucked in between large office buildings. He killed the engine while I sat there stunned in the passenger seat.

"In what world would he ever be my date?"

"In this one, love. He can give you the details when you get inside."

"He's here? At the spa?"

My hands flew to my bare face. I had no makeup on, my hair was twisted up in a messy bun, and my yoga pants had seen better days. I'd been on my way to have a massage, not to see Deacon freaking Miller.

"What could you be thinking, Ollie?"

He chuckled. "I'm thinking people went nuts after your kiss on stage and they're still talking about it. So why not capitalize on it by spending time together?"

"You want me to take the hottest rock star in the world as my fake date?"

"Why don't you start by talking to him about it first. Off you go."

"Off I go," I muttered, getting out of the car and thinking it was easy for him to say. His legs weren't shaking.

If I wasn't nervous, I might've appreciated the tranquility of the soft sage and lavender colors of the spa lobby. Glancing around, I had no idea how this meeting was supposed to take place. It wasn't as if Deacon was there waiting on one of the sofas.

"Good morning," the receptionist greeted with a big smile on her face.

"Good morning. My name is Andrea Foreman. I have a massage appointment."

Her face didn't change at hearing my name. Was she unaware I was here to meet Deacon? Maybe Ollie had been mistaken. Then I was shown to my room, and there the rock star was, sitting in the corner chair.

Damn. He was even hotter than I'd remembered. Dressed casually in ripped jeans and a vintage Jimmi Hendrix T-shirt, he reduced me to simply staring. Although I'd recently seen him on stage, I'd been in such shock at the time I hadn't taken in all the sexy details. Like the way his brown hair was styled in "rock-star chic," longer on top and tousled in an effortless way.

His sea-blue eyes reflected brightly beneath dark lashes, but it was the scruff on his baby face which truly sold the rocker image.

I unconsciously held my breath until my lungs demanded air. Slowly drawing in a breath, I forced my gaze not to focus on his tattooed, muscular arms.

"Hi, Andi."

"Nobody calls me that," I blurted out.

His grin was straight out of any woman's fantasy. "Perhaps you'd do me the honor of letting me be the first."

His charm factor was off the charts, making it difficult to deny him the simple request. "We'll see."

Glancing back toward the door, I wondered if the massage therapist would interrupt us and whether I'd be relieved or disappointed when she did.

"I told them I needed ten minutes to speak with you before they begin your session. Hopefully Ollie told you I was here, and I'm not coming off as a total stalker."

"He did."

"Have a seat, please." He motioned toward the other chair with his hand.

I couldn't help tugging at my faded blue T-shirt. It had seen better days.

His eyes tracked my movements. "I apologize if I'm making you uncomfortable."

"No, no, it's fine." But the way he held my gaze as if he was attempting to read my thoughts did fray my nerves. "What did you want to talk to me about?"

"Straight to the point. I like it."

"It's a new skill I'm trying out." I'd no longer pretend I was comfortable with the boundaries other people set for me.

"I thought perhaps we could help each other out. You as my date to my stepbrother's wedding tonight, and I as your plus-one for your season wrap party tomorrow night."

"Why would you bring someone you don't know to a wedding?" And why take a date at all, for that matter, if there was no one he was currently seeing?

He leaned forward, his knees almost touching mine. "I need to sell the fact I'm in a romantic relationship. Given the buzz around our kiss, it wouldn't be far-fetched to believe that I could be starting one with you."

My brows shot up. "Why do you 'need' people to believe you're in a romantic relationship?"

He exhaled harshly. "My ex is marrying my stepbrother and seems to believe I still harbor feelings for her. By showing up with a date, especially one the public are excited to see me with, it sends a message."

His ex was marrying into his family. And I thought dealing with my ex was bad. "Do you have to go to the wedding at all?"

"No, but my mom asked me to, and although I think Bryce is an idiot for marrying Nina, he's a good guy. If I don't show up, she'd tell everyone it's because I couldn't bear to watch the woman I love marry someone else."

Although there was a healthy dose of sarcasm in his last sentence, I had to ask. "And do you still love her?"

"I never did." He sighed, softening his blunt response. "We dated all of three months, and most of it was long distance. I was honest and upfront when I realized her feelings were developing into something deeper than mine." He paused. "And I'll be honest with you. I'm leaving Monday for Australia."

"In other words, we fake it for one weekend only."

"There'd be nothing fake about our spending time together, Andi, but yes, that time would be limited."

Damn, the way he dropped the newly adopted nickname hit me below the belt. There were many reasons to say no, but a brief escape from reality would be refreshing.

"How would we leave things? For the press?" The last thing I needed was more breakup drama in my life.

"We'd tell the press we had an incredible weekend hanging out together and that we're friends who will stay in touch—which I hope would be true."

It sounded amazing on the surface, but Saturday would potentially be an emotional shitshow for me. "Seeing my soon-to-be ex-husband with his new mistress and not at all concerned about my feelings is bound to put me straight out of the running for date of the year."

"All the more reason to have someone there with you. Although I have to ask you the same question you asked me. Why go to the season wrap party at all? Can't you fight the contract?"

"I think it'll be easier to go to the party and then be done with the show forever." Ollie had tried to find a way for me to get out of that part of the signed agreement, but ultimately it would involve lawyers, and I already had one too many these days. I didn't need another attorney running up an hourly bill rate.

"You won't return for another season?"

"Not a chance." I'd done the show out of love for Jeff. For the first time since the bombshell of his cheating had dropped, a weight started to lift. I would no longer have to allow my life to be chronicled for everyone to watch.

"Although Ollie tells me I should wait to tell production I'm leaving for good until after I do an exclusive interview—that is, if I decide to do the interview at all."

Chapter Six
DEACON

I had no clue how much money Andrea made or what kind of camera time she got on *City of Angels*, but it was guaranteed the producers would hope to play up this marital drama next season and would do all that they could to get her locked into another contract. So once they found out she had no intention of returning, they would manipulate the storyline any way they saw fit and with zero care for her welfare.

"Ollie gives good advice."

She chuckled. "Is that your way of saying I should agree to fake date you?"

"I think it would be fun to spend time together."

She hesitated for the briefest of seconds. "I have questions."

The fact she wasn't jumping at the opportunity to be my date was refreshing. "Ask away."

"What time is this wedding tonight?"

"Seven o'clock."

She sighed. "Is it black tie?"

I nodded, watching her anxiety rise. At this point she appeared on the verge of telling me no way in hell.

Taking out my phone, I typed a quick text. "Ollie will schedule someone to do your hair and makeup and give you a few dress options to choose from. They can come to your place, or you're welcome to get ready at mine."

She chewed on her adorable bottom lip, causing me almost to groan out loud at the inadvertently sexy action.

"Your place would be better."

That made sense considering she still shared a house with her ex. "I'll have a car pick you up at your place at two o'clock. That'll allow you to finish your appointment here and get home. You'll have plenty of time then at my place to get hair and makeup done before we head to the venue."

Not that she needed help with her hair or makeup. From the moment she'd walked into the room, I'd been struck by how beautiful she was even with her face devoid of makeup or any artificial enhancers. This was especially true when she smiled. And I intended to ensure she did a lot of that this weekend.

"What do you say, Andi? Wanna make some plans for the weekend?"

She blew out a breath and held out her hand. "All right. I'm in."

There it was again. An unmistakable pulse of energy the moment my hand touched hers. But unlike my actions up on stage, I pulled away quickly. We'd agreed to fake dating, nothing else.

I left Andrea to her massage appointment, slipped out the back door of the spa and into the passenger seat of Ollie's SUV.

"I take it things went well if you have me booking a glam squad for this afternoon?" he asked immediately.

"Thankfully, she agreed to the weekend." I wasn't sure why I'd been anxious she might not. After all, I was a grown man who could go to the wedding by myself. But the thought of spending more time with her made me happy.

"You tell her about Nina being the bride?"

"Of course. I want her to be aware of what she's getting into. Now tell me what I'm getting into on Saturday? How can I best support her through what's bound to be hell at the wrap party where her husband will be with his mistress?"

He sighed. "Honestly, it's bad enough Jeff hates Andrea getting sympathy and him being painted the bad guy, but he will absolutely lose his shit at seeing she has moved on so quickly—and with you, of all people. His ego won't be able to handle the idea of her trading up. Mark my words, he'll throw a tantrum. Good news is he'll show his true colors. Bad news is he'll attempt to demolish her self-esteem on his way down."

My temper flared in just thinking about it.

"Best thing you can do is keep your cool and turn on your charm."

"And the best thing she can do?"

"Not engage. Make it clear he doesn't have any claim to her life any longer. They might have the house and legal affairs to sort out, but she doesn't need to grant him any more of her time."

"She have a good divorce attorney?"

His pause had me worried. "The best are overpriced, so she went with one who is more reasonable. Time will tell as to how good he is."

I had to remind myself this wasn't my business. Andrea

was a virtual stranger, and she'd figure out her divorce the same as countless others out there had done. "Guess I'll see you at my house later too?"

He smiled. "Of course. Wouldn't want to miss the beginning of the revenge weekend."

Chapter Seven
ANDREA

"There's no way I can wear this." I couldn't believe the slinky dress fit, but evidently I'd shed a few pounds over the last couple weeks.

Ollie glanced up from his phone and smiled as I walked out of the bedroom that had been converted into a dressing room for me in Deacon's spacious Los Angeles home.

Ollie was already at Deacon's place, along with Portia for wardrobe and a man named Miguel for makeup and hair. The goal was to pick out two dresses from the rack that had been provided. One was for the wedding and one was for the party tomorrow night. I'd started working on the outfit for tomorrow since Portia thought it might be the harder one to choose. She wasn't wrong. I'd been through four choices already. Revenge was complicated.

She pulled at the straps holding up the black silk dress. With its plunging back and slit up the side, the garment left nothing to the imagination except for the question of what kind of underwear I could possibly wear with it.

"It's the perfect fuck-you dress for your cheating bastard of an ex-husband," she remarked in a thick accent, taking pins from her mouth and tagging up the hem as well as the waistline. "I can do alterations tonight and drop it off tomorrow morning."

"It's not something I'd normally wear."

Portia, my new confidence booster in blunt form, paused with the pins between her teeth. "Exactly the point."

"It's a statement dress," Ollie offered, picking out some black shoes with red bottoms and straps that wrapped around the ankles. The outfit was ridiculously sexy even if I wasn't.

Could I do it? Could I pull it off? Jeff had always been adamant I dress conservatively, like it was part of my brand as a married woman not to be overly sexy. It was laughable considering he'd left me for a woman who constantly had her body on display in barely there clothes. "All right. Let's do the black dress for tomorrow night."

Now that I had my revenge outfit, the next order of business was to pick out a classy outfit for the wedding tonight. I shimmied into a beautiful A-line chiffon lace cocktail dress of slate blue with sparkle along the bodice and stepped out of the bedroom. That's when I discovered Ollie and Portia were no longer my only audience.

Looking as though he'd come directly from the gym, Deacon dragged his gaze over me from head to toe, causing my cheeks to heat at the scrutiny. Since the weddings I'd previously attended had been much more casual, I asked, "Is this okay for tonight?"

His eyes met mine. "It's perfect."

He moved to greet Portia with a kiss on the cheek. She quickly walked into the bedroom and came out holding two garment bags. "I have the gray suit for tonight and the black slacks with the dark blue collared shirt for tomorrow, Deacon."

He took both in hand. "Great. I'll get showered and changed."

I had just finished with makeup and had my hair in an updo with soft tendrils left loose to frame my face when Deacon walked into the room in his gray suit.

Although it appeared perfectly tailored to fit his body, Portia went over and immediately started tugging on the sleeves and running her hands over the lines of the shoulders. Although she'd done the same to me, I couldn't help the kernel of jealousy over the way she was touching him with such familiarity.

Stupid for more reasons than I could count.

Miguel stepped back, allowing me to take in my reflection in the mirror he'd set up on the dining table. That's when I discovered the man was an absolute artist.

He'd made the dark circles under my eyes disappear and managed to make me look sophisticated and, dare I say, pretty. It was such a great boost to my confidence even if the whole wedding date was pretend.

"Thank you," I whispered, giving him a small smile and choking back my emotion.

Miguel, who turned out to be a fan of the show, grinned. "Tonight you are beautiful butterfly; tomorrow you will be ferocious tiger."

Ollie chuckled. "Yes, indeed. Now, then, we're going to get packed up and leave you two some time to get acquainted."

Within minutes, my mobile Cinderella squad and PR agent had left us completely alone in the house.

"You hungry?" Deacon walked into the bedroom where I was sitting and waiting for my nails to dry.

"Won't there be food at the wedding?"

He chuckled. "That's hours away, and I'm a growing boy."

"And you plan to cook something now?"

He smirked. "The closest version to cooking that I can manage without complaint. Come on, I'll show you the kitchen."

I'd seen it briefly when arriving but now took in all the details: the top-of-the-line chrome appliances, the beautiful white marble countertops. It showed like a model kitchen, probably because he didn't live here long enough to accumulate clutter.

"When I moved in, I had the kitchen and the bathrooms redone."

"They're beautiful. Do you spend much time here?" Modern and clean lines seemed to be his style.

"I'm in LA a few times a year to see my mom or when I have to meet with my record label." He went to the refrigerator and pulled out deli meat and cheese.

I watched as he methodically assembled two sandwiches. It was strange to see one of the world's biggest rock icons do something mundane.

"You prefer ham or turkey?"

"I should probably pass." I was hungry, but it could wait.

"Are you a vegetarian? Because I can make you a veggie version."

I fanned out my dark red—never would've picked this color before—nails. "No, but I don't want to smudge these."

A grin slowly slid across his face. "Easily solved."

He sliced the sandwich in half and held one of the halves up for me.

"I'll hold it, and you take as many bites as you like."

Chapter Eight
DEACON

What started out as an idea to keep any food from ruining Andrea's manicure turned into an unexpected seduction. Each small bite she took caused her to make a tantalizing hum of pleasure. Jesus, even watching her chew was turning me on.

After three bites and a drink of water, she stepped back. "I should've asked: do I look okay for tonight?"

"You look beautiful." I had been struck by how stunning she was when I'd first walked into the room, but I hadn't wanted our audience to discover how attracted I was to her. "Are you nervous?"

"A little. Although I'm sure this is hard to believe considering I put my life on reality TV, I'm more introvert than extrovert."

I finished off her half of the sandwich and glanced at her before starting on the other one. "Most days, I'd rather be home than out too."

Her brows rose. "I wouldn't have pictured you a homebody, but I suppose a public image is never reflective of the real person."

"No, it isn't. Admittedly, in my twenties, I spent my fair share of time at parties and had more late nights than I could count. But acting like a human garbage disposal for fast food and alcohol took a toll. I started running out of breath during concerts, had trouble sleeping, and was on the edge of burnout. After turning thirty, I cleaned up my diet and started working out regularly. As a result, I turned out my best albums and tours to date. More energy, less anxiety, and found myself more present in everything I do."

I had no idea what had me oversharing like this considering I typically kept things to myself, having learned the hard way how easily things got leaked to the press. But something about Andrea made me trust her.

"What a wonderful turning point for you. Not everyone gains that type of self-awareness to recognize when it's time for a life change."

She laid her hand on mine, the depths of her sincerity reflected in her eyes. Jesus, Ollie hadn't been joking when he'd said she was special.

"Do you plan on staying in LA?" I queried, curious to find out more about this woman.

Her hand retracted. "Not any longer than I have to, but I imagine it'll take a while to get through the divorce and settle our assets."

"You think he'll draw it out?"

"He's already gone around the house putting sticky notes on all the things he's claiming, so yeah."

"Seriously?" How fucking petty could someone be especially when he'd been the one to turn her life upside down.

"Afraid so, but can I ask you a favor?"

Usually when someone asked me for a favor, it involved money or an introduction to someone in the business, yet when Andrea asked, I didn't hesitate to say, "Name it."

"Tonight we don't talk about my ex or the impending ridiculous fight over my sofa pillows."

My lips twitched into a grin. "Deal, but unfortunately I can't promise you the same reprieve this evening."

"Speaking of which, what should I expect?"

I sighed, wishing we could skip the wedding and just stay here instead. We'd turn on a movie, order pizza, and sit around talking. "On the bright side you'll meet my mom. She'll be over the moon that I'm bringing a date and will probably have twenty questions for you. My stepfather, Rob, will talk to you about his smoker and how he's perfecting his barbeque sauce for ribs. My stepbrother, Bryce, will be happy to see you because, although he wants to believe his fiancée is madly in love with him, that means I've moved on."

"And Nina will be a wild card?"

"Wild card is an understatement. She knows I'm bringing a plus-one, but my guess is she assumes it's my manager or a friend."

"She'll be jealous to see you with me?"

"Considering it's her wedding day, I sincerely hope not. My goal isn't to make her jealous; it's to quell any rumors that I'm still hung up on her. Don't worry. We won't spend long at the reception."

I appreciated that his motivation was only to squash rumors and not make his ex react to him having a date.

He put all of the fixings for the sandwiches away before straightening his tie. "You ready for night one?"

Chapter Nine
ANDREA

Was I ready for tonight? Doubtful, but I was dressed up for the occasion, and there was no turning back now.

"Ready." As far as my rock-star fantasies were concerned, holding out my hand for a fist bump was not on the list. But here I was doing it anyhow like a total idiot. Nothing said fake dating more than a lame fist bump.

He smirked after meeting my knuckles. "Let's go to a wedding."

I'd expected a mega star like Deacon to have a driver, so I was surprised when he led me to his garage. "You're driving?"

"Any chance I get. Security will be staffed at the venue which means it's just the two of us for now."

"You need security wherever you go?"

"In major cities, yes. Back in Australia, no."

He ran his hand over the sleek lines of his black sports car as though he'd missed it.

"She's beautiful." I had no idea what kind of car it was, but she came across as expensive.

"Wait until you feel her run." He opened up the passenger side door and took my hand to assist me into the low, leather seat.

Jesus, never had I ever been turned on by the smell of a car. But between the rich leather and the faint smell of his cologne, my senses were overwhelmed. And that was before Deacon slid into the driver's seat looking like the sexiest man alive in his well-tailored suit. The juxtaposition of his formal wear with the peek of tattoos along the sliver of skin showing at his wrists was enough to make my head spin.

He glanced over. "You okay?"

Not at all. Because in this scenario of fake dating, I'd never considered the intimacy of spending time with him.

"Yeah. Fine." My voice didn't sound the least bit convincing.

He reached over and took my hand. "I'd tell you not to be nervous tonight, but it doesn't work that way, does it?"

"No, I don't suppose it does." How ironic that the source of my anxiety was now holding my hand in the small confines of the car. Although the thought of meeting so many strangers tonight was less than comforting, doing so would at least be a reprieve from the intensity of being alone with Deacon.

"If I forget to say it later, thank you for coming with me tonight."

His thoughtfulness wasn't lost on me. "If I forget to tell you, I've smiled more today than I have in weeks, so thank you."

He raised my knuckles to his mouth, and I watched with wide eyes as he skimmed his lips over them. "You deserve to smile again."

Relief-appointment—my new marinated word for both relief and disappointment. The sensation hit me when he let go of my hand in order to start the car and pull out of the garage.

As soon as we were on the road, he started the conversation again. "Ollie mentioned you have a dog?"

"I do. Her name is Callie. She's a shepherd mix I rescued about two years ago, and she's such a love."

"He who shall not be named won't fight you for her, will he?"

I appreciated the way he danced around mentioning my ex. "She's always been my dog, and it's my name on the adoption certificate, so my lawyer believes it'll be fine. But who knows?" Not that I'd show my cards at this point, but I'd give up every material possession I owned in order to keep Callie. "Do you have any pets back in Australia?"

"I wish. But my life hasn't lent itself to that since I'm frequently on the road. But I have twenty-three acres there, so I always thought it would be nice to have some animals once things slow down."

"You should get mini cows. They're adorable. And maybe some chickens, oh, and a whole lot of dogs of course."

He chuckled. "Sounds like you'd prefer to move out of the city."

"I really would. I'm fond of the idea of starting a sanctuary where I can take in rescue animals."

"Where is home originally?"

"Small town in Kansas, but I don't see myself moving back. It feels like…"

"Failure," he finished, empathy in his expression.

"Yeah. I guess it's because my ex and I grew up there together, so it wouldn't feel as though I was getting away from him or the memories. Or the expectations. Even my mom thinks I should fight for him—as if a second chance for a cheater should be automatic."

He whipped his head toward me. "Are you thinking about it?"

"Not at all. But she lives on the same street as his parents, and it would be easier for her if we were back together. That kind of pressure is not what I want to hear every day. Guess you could say I crave a fresh start when I leave LA. Luckily, my job is remote, making it possible to work from anywhere."

"You kept your day job?"

I laughed at his surprise. "Yeah, I'm a programmer."

"Cool. What sort of things do you program?"

"I do website design for online retail stores. My company contracts with small businesses, and I work on a project-by-project basis. The hours are flexible, and I enjoy it."

"I should have you update my website."

"Say the word, fake date, and we'll make it happen."

He chuckled, and I found myself relaxing with him in the car as we navigated through traffic. Up until the point he put on the radio and began to sing along with the song. Damn. No autotune for this guy; he was the real deal, talent pouring out with every sexy note.

"Tell me about when you started singing?" I could've read up on him, but I'd wanted him to tell me his own story.

"I started singing in church when I was young, and the choir director encouraged my mom to get me lessons. By high school, which oddly enough is only a few miles from here, I'd started a band, and by my sophomore year of college, I'd dropped out for a record deal."

"What's your favorite part of it?"

"Writing songs. Even if I didn't sing another note, I'd still need to create art."

"Australia is the place that inspires you?"

"It does. Because once I'm there, people wave and say

hello, but they don't treat me like a celebrity when I'm out getting groceries or running errands. Something about the anonymity brings me down to earth and allows me to get into my humble, creative space."

"I would imagine being out on tour and traveling from city to city you don't get much of a chance to be by yourself. Probably nice to have an empty room and silence to keep you company."

Chapter Ten
DEACON

She'd nailed exactly why I was anxious to get back to Australia. I found myself tempted to tell her she should visit. Stupid. An invitation like that would send her the ultimate mixed message. My retreat there was my escape, not something I shared with anyone else.

Checking the GPS, I grimaced at the short distance remaining and the clock running down to the start of the difficult part of the evening. "Five minutes until showtime. Ready?"

She sat up and checked her makeup in the visor mirror. "Guess so. How will you introduce me?"

Good question. "Best to be vague and simply say you're my date."

My sigh filled the car when we got to the gate of the private entrance. A large number of fans were already lining the road, and they went wild upon seeing me pull up. Cameras flashed from every angle. It wouldn't have surprised me to learn Nina had called to have them all here.

Andrea crouched low in her seat. "If they see me, I'm

sure they'd have plenty to say about you bringing me here given my marital status."

"I don't give a fuck about what people think or say. What I care about is how you're feeling." After passing the gate, we cruised up the private driveway and pulled into the valet area. Before opening my door, I turned to her. "And that means if this becomes too much for you, you say the word. Okay?"

She nodded, her doe eyes making me want to throw the car back in drive and take her far away from the hurt, the unfair judgment, and the life she'd thought she'd had only to be betrayed by the one person who should've protected her the most.

The sound of the valet opening my driver's side door interrupted, causing us both to enter back into the real world. She pasted on a smile while I thanked the valet and hurried around the other side in order to assist Andrea out of the car.

The way she gazed up at me, with her lips parted, made my heart beat up into my throat. When the hell was the last time I'd been nervous with a woman? Yet here I was, almost giddy at the excuse to touch her. The shake in her hand had me pulling her close. "You're stunning, and I'm proud to have you as my date."

There it was. A genuine smile pulled from her lips. "Thank you."

We were at the Vibiana, a former cathedral turned event venue in the heart of downtown Los Angeles. I nodded at my two guys, part of the security team I'd hired to ensure this occasion stayed private and the public stayed outside the gate.

We were greeted by a woman in a business suit wearing a headset and a smile. "Mr. Miller, this way, please."

"Wow, this is lovely," Andrea whispered, looking around the historic halls as we were led to a large courtyard that had been decorated for the ceremony.

"It is." My mother had told me all about the place over the last couple of weeks, obviously excited to be involved in the planning.

Our guide led us to the rows of white chairs. There were a few people already seated, but most were standing around talking since we still had some time before the ceremony. Surveying the courtyard, I didn't see any familiar faces.

"You can take any two seats in this row when it's time," the usher said. "The bar is open in the back, and the ceremony will start in approximately thirty minutes."

"Thank you." Once we were alone, I found myself taking Andi's hand again. What could I say? I enjoyed an excuse to touch her. "Want something to drink?"

"No, thank you. How are you doing?"

Her question took me off guard. I was accustomed to powering through obligations without anyone caring about my feelings. "I'm fine. If anything, having you here with me has made it easy to forget I'm counting the minutes."

"We can stay as long as you'd like."

"I promised my mom I'd stay until after dinner. Then I say we blow this place and get milkshakes at the Take 'n Shake."

Her eyes sparkled. "Sounds like it'll be the best part of our date. What flavor you going for?"

I was about to answer when a woman dressed in a long gown approached. I assumed she was a bridesmaid. "Hi, I'm Jen, and I'm sorry to interrupt, Deacon. Your mother sent me to have you come back for a quick word."

"Oh, okay." I turned to Andi. "Want to come meet my mom?" I hadn't introduced a woman to my mother since high school when I'd needed her to drive us, yet introducing Andrea to her felt natural.

"Oh, um, she indicated she needed a private word with you," Jen interrupted, seeming embarrassed to have to clarify.

Andrea squeezed my fingers. "It's all right. Go talk with her. I'll be fine."

"Okay." I followed Jen down one of the side corridors. She seemed nervous, so I started casual conversation. "How's your day been?"

"Fine. Um, follow me."

She led me into a large room, and through a door opening off of it. I started to feel like I'd been taken into a maze, and when I walked into a large dressing room, I recognized I'd been duped. This was the bridal suite. Jen didn't stick around but scurried back out the door we'd come in from. "Sorry," she whispered.

Despite having a good idea what was going on, I still stood there in shock when Nina came out from behind the elaborate dressing screen wearing only her bridal-white corset and stockings with lacy garters.

She'd always been a striking woman with her long blond hair and svelte, supermodel frame, but my dick didn't stir. Instead I was anxious to get back to Andrea with her big green eyes and delightful smiles. "What do you want, Nina?"

Her injected lips attempted to make a pout. "How can you be so cruel?"

"It's your wedding day, and yet you're standing in front of me in your underwear. Why?" I already knew the answer, but I hoped if she were forced to say it, she'd realize just how crazy she sounded.

"Because this is your last chance." She put her hands on her hips to emphasize the ridiculous ultimatum.

My head was already shaking no. "It's not going to happen. I came here in support of Bryce, who loves you and believes you're ready to spend the rest of your life with him.

If that's not the case, then you owe it to tell him that before walking down the aisle."

If she had any moral compass, she would feel guilty, but instead her temper snapped. "You don't get to tell me what to do. But mark my words, you will regret losing me."

Now wasn't the time to tell her how much I wouldn't. Instead I wanted to get out of here as quickly as possible, especially since I could see Nina was ready to cause a real scene. "All the best to you."

Outside the suite's door, Jen had been joined by another bridesmaid. Both of them stood in the hall wide-eyed as I strode out and didn't bother to look back. Great, I could already imagine the rumors. I headed straight to the courtyard where more people had gathered.

Andi remained in her seat. "Hi," she greeted with a big smile only to have it falter. "What's wrong?"

"Nothing, now that I'm back." My hand automatically took hers. This was quickly becoming a habit.

Her eyes searched my face. "Everything all right with your mom?"

"It actually wasn't her I was led back to see," I whispered, my adrenaline pumping from the confrontation.

"The bride?"

"Afraid so."

"Oof. I gather it wasn't to thank you for coming and she wishes you all the best because her upcoming wedding day is the happiest day of her life, and she only wants everyone else to feel the same?"

My lips twitched in a smile. "You'd be correct."

"Will you tell your stepbrother?"

"When they started dating, I tried to warn Bryce about her, and he accused me of being jealous. A conversation today would be disastrous." I was tempted to leave.

"Could be she's hoping you'll cause a scene by leaving and twist it around like you tried to prevent the wedding and didn't get your way."

Andrea's perception was spot on, and it immediately brought me a sense of much-needed calm. My ex wanted drama, and I refused to give it to her. "Thank you for reminding me not to react."

She squeezed my hand. "I can be your calming goat today, and you can be mine tomorrow."

"My what?"

"Calming goat. You know, 'baa.'"

A chuckle burst from my lips. She was adorable, and her random outburst allowed the residual tension to float away.

Chapter Eleven
ANDREA

Had I really just bleated at *People Magazine*'s sexiest man of the year?

Yes, yes I had.

That was one dorky fist bump and one humiliating "baa." Someday perhaps it would be a funny story, but meanwhile I could feel my face burning red.

"What is a calming goat exactly?"

In for a penny, in for a pound. "Racehorses are known to spook easily, so sometimes they introduce them to goats since the goats can calm them." How I knew this, I couldn't remember, but he nodded sagely as if absorbing the information for future use.

Do not baa again at the man. Do not baa again.

Perhaps I was the one who needed the calming goat because I had felt my temperature rising ever since he'd taken my hand after returning from the bridal suite, and now it was only getting worse with this ridiculous word salad I was serving up. Needless to say, my anxiety was spiking into unknown territory.

He rubbed his thumb on the inside of my wrist, causing

shivers to snake down my spine. "Sounds like the goats could complement your mini cows."

People started to take their seats around us, giving me a reprieve from any further goat conversation.

A quartet of string instruments to the left started to play, and the seats began to fill. An older woman with chic, short blond hair was led down the aisle by a man in a suit who must have been her husband. Given her stunning blue eyes, there was no doubt she was Deacon's mother.

As if confirming this hypothesis, she flashed a beaming smile in the direction of her son and took a seat in the front row in front of us beside her husband. Next came the men in traditional black-and-white tuxes who took up positions to the sides of the officiant, who stood in the center of an elevated stage.

My gaze focused on the groom. Bryce was a decent-looking man, but couldn't have been more the opposite of Deacon. It was as if one was the sexy bad boy, and the other was his clean-cut, drive-a-Toyota-Prius accountant.

We all got to our feet once the wedding march started to play. The bride began the walk down the aisle with an older man in a tux who must have been her father. She was stunning. As in grace-a-magazine-cover stunning, with her tall, statuesque frame and long blond hair curled down her back. Take a Barbie bride doll, and she was a dead ringer.

The besotted groom lit up like a kid on Christmas morning when he laid eyes on her. I felt a stab of empathy for the guy given he had no clue that just minutes ago she'd been ready to call the entire thing off if Deacon had only said the word.

Watching this love triangle unfold in real time left me feeling sad for him and angry at her. No one deserved to be made a fool of.

Deacon, as if sensing my mood shift, squeezed my hand in support. We seated ourselves again, and I didn't miss the way Nina's gaze swung to us, immediately laser-focused in on Deacon, and flicked to me and down to where our hands were joined. Even from twenty feet away, I could feel the flames of jealousy.

Then she appeared to remember this was her wedding, and she should concentrate on the man she was about to marry. She refocused and pasted on a smile.

I'd never attended a more excruciating ceremony. Not that it was long if measured by the clock, but the feeling of watching a man about to make one of the biggest mistakes of his life slowed the minutes. Or perhaps what made it feel tense was wondering if at any moment she'd bolt.

Once it was over, I let out a long breath. As the newly dubbed husband and wife walked down the aisle, Bryce looked as though he'd won the biggest prize, and Nina appeared annoyed that Deacon hadn't stood up and shouted "objection."

"That was painful," Deacon whispered under his breath so only I could hear.

He could say that again.

Around us, people began to stand up. Deacon's mom turned around and smiled at her son. "So happy you're here."

He leaned in and gave her a hug. "Nice to see you."

After pulling back, he made introductions. "Andrea, this is my mom, Vivian, and her husband, Rob."

They both flashed warm smiles my way.

"Nice to meet you both."

"You as well— Oh, we're being summoned for photos." She paused. "Don't suppose you want to do some family pics?"

Deacon chuckled. "Not a chance, but I'll find you at the reception, and we'll ensure we get one together."

She seemed satisfied with his compromise. "Deal. See you both in a bit."

As people started to file out of the rows and into the beautiful reception hall, Deacon took my hand and pulled me down a different hallway where we could be alone.

"You look ready either for a drink or to bolt," I remarked.

His smile came quickly. "Both would be fantastic, but we'll settle on the drink, a picture with my mother, a quick meal, and then we can split if that's all right with you?"

The way he always checked to see how I felt about things was endearing. "I'm here for you tonight for however long you wish to stay."

"Thank you." He took a deep breath before offering his arm.

The indoor reception hall was beautifully decorated in white and silver. The result was both elegant and sophisticated. I could only imagine what an extravagant wedding like this must have cost.

We were greeted by black-tie servers who proffered trays of appetizers and champagne to the guests who milled around while the bridal party took photos outside. It was cute how people wanted to meet Deacon and say hello without being obvious or making him uncomfortable.

Deacon was gracious and took the time to introduce me as his date to everyone he spoke with. I witnessed the curious glances in my direction, making it clear they all wondered who I was and the status of our relationship. My date kept his hand in mine or at the small of my back, the perfect gentleman at all times.

When the main doors opened and the bridal party came in, the DJ started spinning music. As the bride and groom made their entrance, I was once again struck by the contrast in their facial expressions. He exuded joy and happiness while she wore a guarded smile. There was no mistaking the way Nina surveyed the room until her eyes collided with Deacon.

Her chin lifted, and her shoulders squared.

"I don't think I've ever seen a bride look quite so, uh, determined," I whispered to him. To do what, I wasn't sure. Make Deacon jealous, seem happy, appear as though she didn't care she'd been rejected? It was like watching a reaction roulette wheel and wondering which emotion it would land on.

"I'm hoping to get out of here without having to speak to her again."

Considering the evil side eye she was giving us, I'd say that possibility was a big fat no.

Luckily we were seated with Deacon's mom and stepfather, making it easy to take photos and have comfortable conversation while the food was being served. At least up until the point his mom asked what should have been a simple question.

"How did you two meet?"

Deacon took my hand under the table which was quickly becoming a habit.

"We share the same PR rep. When he took her to my last concert, I pulled her up on stage and kissed her in front of thousands of chanting fans. Afterward, I couldn't stop thinking about her and kept pestering her until she agreed to go out with me. Now here we are."

My mouth nearly hung open before I remembered to play my part, gulping a swallow of wine and smiling at his explanation.

"Nice to see you doing the chasing for once," Vivian

quipped with a wink. "Are you still planning to leave for Australia on Monday?" She sounded hopeful he might stay local.

"I am."

He gave no further explanation for his impending departure. While I was relieved he wasn't expanding on the lie, I did feel disappointed at this reminder that I'd never see him again.

Actually, scratch that. I'd see him plenty. On television, in ads, and on covers of magazines, but I wasn't delusional enough to believe we'd stay in touch.

After a delicious meal of salmon and risotto, the DJ announced that it was time for the bride and groom's first dance.

Meanwhile, a large man in an all-black suit and wearing an earpiece came up to have some words with Deacon.

He sighed as the man walked away. "Evidently, we're here for a while longer. Security is handling some overzealous photogs who jumped the fence."

"Sorry." I knew he was anxious to leave.

Others had now joined the dance floor. At the start of the second slow song, Deacon tugged on my hand. "The delay could have one benefit. Dance with me?"

Had any woman ever said no to such an invitation? "I'd love to."

I could thank my mother for ten years of dance classes so that I could now avoid stepping on Deacon's toes. Being in his arms left me with a floaty, tingling feeling.

After a couple minutes, he asked, "How would you sum up the evening thus far?" A smirk played on his lips.

My gaze slid to my left, where the bride was throwing daggers at my profile. "Your mom is lovely, your stepfather seems nice, and yes, obsessed with barbeque. I feel bad for your stepbrother, dislike the bride despite never having shared a word with her, oh, and the salmon with risotto was tasty."

He threw his head back with laughter, the action causing more attention to focus on us. "I can't begin to thank you enough for coming tonight. You were the bright spot."

It was amazing how comfortable I'd become with Deacon and how well we were getting along. Perhaps there was something to be said for having clear expectations regarding what this was and, more importantly, what it wasn't. "You're welcome. Oh, and incoming."

"Fucking hell," he muttered. With the song over, the bride and groom were making a beeline toward us.

"Hi, Deacon. Thanks for coming today," greeted Bryce, offering his hand to shake.

"Congratulations to you both. It was a beautiful wedding. Let me introduce you. This is Andrea—"

"I was telling Bryce how we spoke before the wedding," Nina interrupted, as if no one needed to know who I was.

Deacon wasn't having it. "As I was saying, this is Andrea. Andrea, this is Bryce and his wife, Nina."

The way he emphasized his familiarity with Bryce and not Nina was an intentional nuance. "Nice to meet you both," I offered.

By the clench of Nina's jaw, the feeling was definitely not mutual.

"You as well, Andrea," Bryce said graciously.

I didn't miss the way Deacon tightened his arm around my waist.

Nina wasn't done with the subject she wanted front and center. "Like I said, Deacon came back to see me before the wedding."

Deacon didn't miss a beat. "Yes, evidently there was a

mix-up when one of the bridesmaids took me to see you instead of to my mother. But luckily Andrea didn't have to wait long for me to return." He smoothed his hand up and down my waist as if to remind his ex of who he was with.

Since her multiple attempts to cause drama had failed, Nina turned to me with a new tactic, venom dripping from her words. "You look familiar, Amanda. Aren't you that reality star's wife who was cheated on?"

Deacon was about to speak, but I gripped his hand. "My name is Andrea, and yes, we're separated due to his infidelity which is definitely not a topic to bring up during a joyous occasion. Congratulations to you two. Beautiful wedding."

Deacon was done with the small talk. "Glad we were able to catch you both before leaving."

"You're leaving? The cake isn't cut yet." Nina sounded almost desperate.

"Yes, apologies, but Andrea and I have limited time together before I leave on Monday, so you understand."

Nina narrowed her eyes and feigned empathy, addressing me. "Don't take it personally when Deacon doesn't invite you to his Australian retreat. He's only invited one of his loves to his special place in all the years he's been living there."

In other words: he'd taken her there.

Deacon stiffened. "Actually, Andrea is joining me there in a few weeks."

Say what now? It was obvious by the way she recoiled that his intention had been to serve notice she'd been replaced. I'd have felt sorry for her if not for the brand-new wedding ring on her left hand.

"With all that he's shared with me about the place, I'm excited to see it in person," I squeaked out, trying to go with the flow of this blatant lie.

"How exciting for you both. Thanks again for coming,

Deacon. It was lovely to meet you, Andrea." Bryce took his bride's arm. "Shall we greet the other guests?"

For a moment I thought Nina might shake off her new husband and make a scene. But it was as if she realized she'd lost this battle. The real question was whether or not she was ready to concede the war.

"Yes, of course. Thank you both for coming."

As soon as they turned, Deacon wasted no time. He led me over to say his goodbyes to his mom and stepfather, paused for a couple photos with some of the other attendees, before he practically jogged me out to the parking lot. He nodded at his security team to indicate he would no longer wait for the rogue photographers to be rounded up.

In my high heels, I was unable to keep up. As if finally noticing, he came to a halt. "Shit, I'm sorry, Andi."

My screaming feet made me wince. "It's all right."

"It really isn't." In an unexpected move, he swept me off my feet and into his arms, striding the last few feet toward the valet. Deacon handed him the ticket as if it was perfectly normal to be balancing a grown woman while doing so. "Better?"

For my feet, yes. For my attraction to him, not at all. "You don't have to carry me."

Oh, sweet baby mini cows, he dropped his face and nuzzled my neck. The sensation of his scruff hit my sensitive skin and sent a shiver down my spine.

I closed my eyes and lost all concept of space and time—until the moment was interrupted with the sound of click, click, click.

Deacon put me down gently, and we turned to see the photog about twenty feet away. Having gotten his pic, the dude waved and jogged down the private drive he'd snuck up for the intrusive photos.

"Guessing that'll be in the tabloids by tomorrow." Taking out his billfold, he tipped the guy who brought around his car. I slid into the passenger side, thanking Deacon for holding the door.

We were quiet as we drove away.

Chapter Twelve

DEACON

My tie didn't stay on past the gate. As I navigated the LA roads, I glanced over at my date.

"I apologize for the comment about you visiting me in Australia." It hadn't been my intent to throw out the lie, but Nina had gotten under my skin, and I hadn't been able to help myself.

"I take it she's the only woman you ever brought there, and she wanted to make sure we all knew it."

"What she failed to mention is that she was never invited. She simply showed up unannounced after I'd told her I'd be gone for four weeks. After she caused a scene at my lack of gratitude for her gesture, I told her we were over."

"Wow. No wonder you wanted to make it sound like I'd be visiting. Hopefully, they can just be happy together."

It was a nice sentiment, but given tonight's antics, I had my doubts.

Andrea took her buzzing phone out of her clutch, frowned, and ended the noise, apparently sending the call to voicemail. But it immediately started buzzing again.

"The ex?"

She looked down as if reading a text, sighing at whatever was there. "Yeah, evidently the picture of us at the valet station didn't wait until tomorrow. It's online now, and Jeff is somehow angry? I don't get it."

"He didn't expect for you to move on so quickly." It pissed me off to hear she might have to deal with this asshole when she got home. "Is he at the house?"

"Not yet, but he said he's on his way."

"You could stay at my house tonight. I have three guest bedrooms you can choose from. Besides, it might be easier to get ready for the wrap party tomorrow at my place." It wasn't the best plan considering I was already fighting my attraction to her, but I hated the alternative where she'd be tangling with her ex.

"What about my dog?"

"Bring her. I have a fenced backyard and plenty of space."

Relief relaxed her features. "You're sure you wouldn't mind?"

"Not at all."

I didn't expect the jealousy that hit me when I walked into Andrea's house. It was tastefully decorated in neutral tones, with both comfortable and showy pieces intermixed. The kitchen appeared newly remodeled with high-end appliances, but it was the cozy towels and mini cow salt and pepper shakers that had me smiling. Her personality definitely showed through.

Glancing around at the other personal touches scattered around that Andrea had gathered with her ex over the years had acid crawling up my throat.

Thankfully, a medium-sized, brown-and-black, long-haired dog came up and broke the mood with a wagging tail and lolling tongue.

"Hello, beautiful." I knelt down to scratch her ears.

"This is Callie. Callie, this is Deacon."

"Nice to meet you." Scanning around the room, I noticed the yellow Post-it notes on almost every piece of furniture. "These are the sticky notes you mentioned?"

She rolled her eyes. "Yep, Jeff's way of calling dibs on the items he wants."

There had to be dozens of notes in this room alone. Looking closer, I could see the block letters, "JEFF." "What kind of petty bullshit is this?" He'd cheated on her and imploded their marriage, and now he wanted to claim things?

"It's his way lately."

Anger coursed through me, but then I remembered our earlier agreement in not talking about him and stopped my thoughts.

She flashed a soft smile. "I'm heading upstairs to pack my things."

"If you point me in the right direction, I'll grab Callie's stuff while you do that."

After packing up Callie's bed, food, and dishes, I led her outside for a quick potty break. Then I loaded her into the small back seat of my car.

Andrea came down the steps carrying a small suitcase and duffle, both of which I took from her hands.

"I can drive my own car over so that Callie's hair won't get on your pretty leather seats."

"It'll be fine. She's already loaded up. Nice shoes, by the way." Although she still wore her formal dress, she'd taken off her heels to put on slippers. It was a look that had me smiling.

"My feet never were great in heels. We should probably go. Jeff will have seen us on the front door camera."

We exited, and she locked the front door. "Camera, you say?"

"Yeah, one of those doorbell cameras."

I didn't think, I just moved, framing her face with my hands and touching my lips to hers. There it was again. The enchantment of our first kiss. However, once again, our time was limited.

Pulling back, I nearly groaned at the way Andi looked, her eyes still closed, her lips open as if she hadn't been ready for the kiss to end. "Let's go." My voice was thick, my entire body humming with adrenaline.

Andi was quiet once she got in the car, and I regretted my impromptu kiss. Here she was having to deal with one immature asshole; she didn't need another one putting on a show instead of considering her feelings.

"I was selfish doing that little stunt for your camera. I'm sorry."

"It's fine. There's a petty part of me who thinks it serves him right."

"It does serve him right. Do you know the woman he's involved with?" So much for my promise. "Never mind. I shouldn't have asked."

"It's fine. Frankly, it's refreshing to know someone hasn't heard all the details from the press. Paula came onto the TV show mid-season when she started dating another cast member. Nobody cared for her at first because she was a little ditzy and would flirt with all the guys. I chalked it up to her being young and naïve, and I guess thirsty for the attention. That was the worst part of being on the show. All of the thirsty people competing for screen time. Anyhow, I befriended her because I thought I could be a calming, big-sister influence. Even convinced the other women on the cast to give her a chance."

"You never suspected the affair?"

"Regrettably, no. Paula even came over for Easter and sat at my dinner table asking questions about our in vitro journey. I thought she was becoming my friend. Little did I know she was only getting close to me in order to spend time with him."

My swallow was painful. "You were trying to get pregnant?"

"Only weeks away from starting the process."

Once again, jealousy flared. I'd spent little time with Andrea but already knew she'd make an incredible mom. "I'm sorry, Andi."

She let out a long breath. "I'm not. I can't imagine trying to co-parent with him. I suppose the timing could be considered a silver lining. Now, then, at the risk of sounding demanding, I do believe someone promised me a milkshake?"

My chuckle filled the car. "Yes, ma'am."

Even something as simple as getting a milkshake turned into a big deal when I was in LA. The moment the cashier realized it was me, the entire staff rushed to the window wanting pictures. I didn't mind, but I was curious as to Andrea's response. It turned out she was an incredible sport, offering to take the photos and air drop them to people's phones.

Once we pulled into my garage, I cut the engine, hit the button to close the door, and turned to Andrea.

"How's the cookies and cream flavor?"

"Delicious. Want a taste?"

I knew she meant to offer her cup, but I took the opportunity to take it straight from her instead. The cold of her lips was a delicious juxtaposition to the heat of the kiss.

"Is this still faking it?" She posed the question in between kisses.

"It hasn't truly been faking it since I kissed you on that stage the first time." I pulled back to cup her chin. "But you've been through so much, and I don't want to hurt you, Andi."

"Kissing you is the best part of the last few days. Whether it's fake or not."

Her grin was contagious, and suddenly we were kissing again. I felt like a teenager making out in my car. The attraction I'd been fighting roared to life, and this time there was no reason to hold back.

The soft mewl in the back of her throat when I kissed her deeper had me anxious to get her inside.

Chapter Thirteen

ANDREA

This was happening. Deacon was kissing me. For real this time with no reason to stop. Except for the fact we were in his car, and my beloved dog was a hostage to the scene.

Deacon seemed to remember we were in the garage at the same time I did. "Stay here a moment."

He was out of the car and around it in seconds to open my door. "I need you out of this dress. You take Callie, and I'll grab her bed. I'll come out and get the rest later."

He took my hand to help me out of the car, reached in to snatch Callie's stuffed bed, and led us into the hallway, through the kitchen, and directly into his master bedroom.

Callie was content at being in the same room as me and lay down on her fluffy bed the moment it was placed on the floor.

"Where were we?" He dove back into our kiss like he couldn't wait another second. I was right there with him. He tasted of milkshake, the combination of chocolate, mint, and him wreaking havoc on my senses.

His fingers worked my zipper, tugging it down my side before sliding the straps off my shoulders. The silk floated down the length of my body to pool on the floor.

"Jesus, you're a vision," he hissed, trailing kisses above the lace of my bra.

Despite my body being totally on board with the idea of getting naked with Deacon, my brain was threatening to interfere. I was anxious about having sex with someone new, and the perfect specimen of a man at that. The more I tried to ignore it, the more my physical reaction kicked in.

"You're shaking," he murmured, pulling back to meet my eyes.

Oh, hell no. I had one weekend, and I planned on enjoying the entire thing. "Ignore it. I know I intend to."

He pressed his forehead against mine. "Talk to me, Andi. Tell me what you're feeling."

Oh, man. How truthful should I be? If he stopped, I wasn't sure I'd ever forgive myself for being honest, but if I didn't put it out there, the anxiety was sure to consume me. "You're the second man I've ever done this with. And I more than want to, but I'm nervous."

"Then let me relax you. Sit on the bed, beautiful."

I took a seat on the luxurious bedding at the foot of the imposing, king-sized bed and watched as he knelt in front of me. Like we were in a fantasy reel, he peeled off his jacket before leaning forward and inhaling my scent over the top of my panties.

"I should shower before you do that." I assumed all men preferred it clean, so imagine my shock when he did a slow shake of his head.

"Do you know how I like my pussy?"

Gulp. "No?"

"I want to eat your pussy smelling and tasting like pussy, not soap. Spread your legs and let me taste you."

Officially the hottest words ever said.

Hooking his thumbs on either side of my underwear, he pulled the scrap of material down my legs, losing it somewhere on the floor. His gaze met mine for a moment before flicking back to my center.

It started with a hot breath and butterfly kisses on the inside of my thighs. I was still shaking, but more from arousal than nerves at this point. Deacon moved slowly, with deliberate strokes of his tongue. "So good," he breathed, teasing me with his tongue, lips, and a nip of his teeth around my delicate skin.

I was convinced I'd die of this delicious torture when he changed it up completely and started the real onslaught, inserting a finger deep inside of me. "You're tight."

One moment I was about to respond with something lame like, "uh-huh," and the next I'd sucked in a breath because he'd taken my clit prisoner between his lips. Meanwhile his tongue showed it no mercy.

His fingers worked me at the same time. Normally, it took me a while to get to such a point, but suddenly I was climaxing with his face buried in my pussy. Upon orgasming with the world's sexiest man, I should have let out a dainty moan with a sophisticated, sensual shudder of my body covered in the perfect misty sheen to add a glow, but not too sweaty.

In reality I screamed so loud that my poor dog came running over to the side of the bed to whine, worried for my safety. "It's okay, girl," I panted out, attempting to sit up but still spasming from the powerful release.

Deacon chuckled at the situation, making my face heat.

"Don't you dare be embarrassed. That was the hottest thing I've ever witnessed."

"The part where I traumatized my dog with my unladylike screams or the portion where your neighbors are probably calling 911 because they suspect a murder next door."

"Ah, lucky for you I've had the windows soundproofed for that very reason." He was so deadpan that my brow arched.

Then he gave it away with laughter. Mine followed, breaking the tension.

But my humor faded the moment Deacon stood up and started to undress. I propped up on my elbows to watch, needing only a bucket of popcorn to make the striptease a real show.

His skin was golden, his tattoos a myriad of colors and designs covering one entire arm in a sleeve and spreading over his pectoral muscle. Dragging my heated gaze down, I salivated at the way his six-pack abs rippled—the type you only saw on TV or in magazines. But these were the real deal.

"In three weeks they'll be gone."

"What do you mean?"

"I mean I'll happily have vacation stomach, where I'm not training every day and watching what I eat. Instead I'll happily be in carb heaven."

"You say that like it's not the sexiest thing you've ever uttered."

Our grins were matching. At least until the point where he whipped off his boxers, and my mouth dropped open.

It was unfair to expect a mega rock star to have a big dick, but Deacon Miller more than delivered. The only thing small was the worry in the back of my mind if he would fit inside of me.

"You're beautiful." My blurt wasn't as bad as bleating at

the man, but it was far from smooth. Sexy bedroom banter was not my forte.

His hand gripped his hardened length. "Yeah, what is it you like the most?"

My gaze was incapable of moving from the sight of him slowly stroking himself in front of me. "Your eyes?" I croaked out.

He threw his head back with laughter. "You're hell on an ego, Andi."

My smile was lopsided. "Yet somehow I think you'll recover."

He moved closer, giving me the chance to run my fingertips over his muscles and incredible ink work. His body was insane.

Stroking his skin, I marveled at the veins in his arms and the way he flexed under my touch. Tentatively, I followed the path of my hands with my mouth. His skin tasted divine. My tongue then skated over his nipple, causing him to inhale sharply. I attempted to move south, but he pulled me back up to his lips.

Good Lord, the man could kiss.

The taste of myself on his tongue only fueled my desire. His guitar-string-calloused fingers stroked my skin, causing delicious tingles from head to toe. I wasn't entirely sure this was reality. How had we gone from fake kisses to having sex?

He wasted no time in pulling a foil packet from his nightstand and slid the condom on with a practiced skill I wouldn't think about.

After climbing on the bed, he spread my legs and notched himself at my opening. Moving forward one delicious inch at a time, he waited for me to adjust to his size.

He swallowed my gasp, a small measure of pain mixed

with the overwhelming pleasure of his kiss. The fullness was a sensation I'd never experienced.

Once he was fully seated, we both let out a collective sigh of relief. I didn't believe the sensation could intensify until he started to move. Slowly at first, his cadence intensified as my body stretched around him. The pleasure was indescribable. Then he went and multiplied it by lifting my hips and pushing deeper.

My hands ran down his biceps and onto his shoulders, feeling the way his entire body flexed with every thrust. The sounds of slapping skin, the smell of his expensive cologne, the lingering taste of his kiss, and him deep inside of me set all of my senses on fire at once.

"I'm getting close." I couldn't believe it was building again so soon after my first orgasm.

"Me too." He reached down between our bodies, circling my clit with devilish precision.

My entire lower half went rigid before I exploded into a million pieces. I was vaguely aware of his growl and the way his body tensed while he ground his climax deep into me. Although my shouts were muted this time around, they were definitely still on the loud side.

"That was incredible," he murmured, sliding out slowly and moving to lie beside me.

"It was," I responded, grateful it hadn't only been in my head.

We lay there awhile, snuggled into one another and allowing our breathing to return to normal. Then, pressing a kiss against my forehead, Deacon climbed out of bed and went toward the bathroom where I assumed he disposed of the condom.

He crawled back into the bed, gathered me close, and

kissed down the curve of my neck. "Do you have any idea how sexy you are?"

I wanted to believe his words. But I'd seen his ex. Tall, thin, with zero curves. As if sensing my doubt, he pulled away the sheet I'd gathered up over my body.

"Don't believe me? Then I'll have to show you."

Yes, please.

Chapter Fourteen

DEACON

I began writing songs when I was twelve and couldn't get a beat or a verse out of my head. Often, I found inspiration in a story, a place, or a feeling, before bringing it all to life with a cadence and rhyming words. The creative process was different for everyone, but mine typically required that I have solitude. I needed to clear my mind of any interference or interruption and hyperfocus on my creative process.

Yet this morning I'd been inspired without any of that. Inspired to pick up my guitar and strum some chords while observing how the morning light showed the light sprinkling of freckles across Andrea's nose and made her skin glow.

When she woke and smiled, it was as if I had my first line writing itself in front of me.

From her kissable lips to her hair all a mess, Andrea Foreman was stunning. The fact she had no idea of this made it intoxicating to watch her confidence flourish.

She sat up in bed, the sheet regrettably covering her gorgeous body. A body I'd ravished twice last night and wasn't nearly done with.

"Sorry if I woke you." My apology didn't ring true given how sexy she looked just now.

The slow smile that played over her lips made my desire for her flare. "Can't think of a better way to wake up."

I set the guitar against the wall and crawled back into the bed, hovering over her so I could dip down to give her a kiss. "I can think of one better way."

If we only had the weekend, I was determined to squeeze as much out of it as I could.

Peeling down the sheet, exposing the full image of her naked form, I paused before letting my eyes wander down in order to lock my gaze on hers. "If you could see a fraction of what I see, you'd walk around my house naked and proud of your body."

I kissed down her chest to make my point and didn't stop until I was hovering over her seriously addictive pussy.

"Let me shower," she protested.

I rolled my eyes. "What did I tell you about how I liked my pussy?"

Her eyes went wide, but I could tell by the trembling of her body that she was turned on. "Tell me, Andi."

"You like it tasting like pussy."

Having her give me my words was such a turn-on. "Damn right. And having it smell like sex and your lips swollen from me being inside of you last night makes it irresistible."

I swiped my tongue through her seam. "Fucking delicious."

"Jesus. I—" She clawed at the sheets when I fastened my lips around her clit and sucked gently.

"You what? Tell me." I was selfish in wanting her words, but I couldn't help it. If her ex was half as greedy as he appeared, it was guaranteed he hadn't been a generous lover.

"I've never felt like this. So consumed and overwhelmed, and, oh, God—"

Her body shuddered when I put two fingers inside of her. There were few things I found more satisfying than playing guitar, but this, this was another level. "You're so wet for me. So ready."

"Yes," she moaned.

"Grab my hair and show me how much you want to come."

Her fingers tangled in my hair, tugging and massaging, demonstrating the depth of her desire. There was nothing hotter than watching her take what she wanted without apology.

I alternated between lazy strokes and rapid licks against her engorged clit while my fingers curved toward her wall to find her G-spot. Relentlessly, I fucked her until she surrendered to my assault, the waves of her orgasm drawn out by the languid way I continued to play with her.

She removed her hand from my head, which was kind of a shame given how I loved feeling her lose control, yanking on my hair while she came in my mouth. Now she sat up on her elbows to stare at me with hooded eyes. Something akin to amazement reflected in their depths.

Because I was only wearing my flannel PJ bottoms with an elastic waist, she was able to make quick work of sliding them off my hips. But I helped, taking them off the rest of the way and throwing them onto the floor. She then reached for me, wrapping her hand around my shaft and gently teasing the head with a circular rub of her thumb.

Next thing I knew, she'd lowered her mouth over the tip. Now it was my turn to gasp at the sensation. It was insanely satisfying to see her peer up at me as if confirming she was doing it correctly.

"Your mouth is heaven." I wasn't exaggerating. She was hot, wet perfection wrapped around me. The way her confidence grew under my compliments was something I'd never experienced. It was addictive, and oh, so satisfying. "That's it, baby, grip me harder."

She did as instructed but then shocked me with an unexpected deepthroat stroke which left me breathless and grabbing for purchase on the bed. "Fucking hell, Andi."

My expletives streamed forth unleashed. The way this woman could go from shy temptress to sexy goddess in the course of a few hours left me in a state of wonder.

Her bobbing threatened to unravel my last shreds of self-control, but when she lapped at my balls, I was done for. "I'm going to come."

I was unsure what to expect, but her taking me deep into her throat and sucking me dry wasn't it. I chanted her name mixed with every curse word I could possibly marinate into my pleasure.

She slowly extricated her mouth from my cock and looked up, wiping at her lips as though she couldn't stand the thought of missing a drop. I nearly came again.

"Good?"

Her question was enveloped in fragility. Taking her face between my hands, I smoothed the dark hair from her face. "Unbelievable."

The combination of her vulnerability and trust left me nearly speechless. This woman had no clue what a gift she was, and suddenly I was hit with the realization that one weekend wouldn't be enough.

Later, I curled her into me, smiling when she dozed off again.

Not at all able to sleep, I climbed out of the bed, took a quick shower, letting Callie outside for a few minutes to do her business. Standing outside with my cup of coffee, I tried not to think about leaving on Monday and how I'd miss Andrea.

The idea was silly. She was an amazing woman, but I barely knew her, and we'd agreed to a weekend, nothing more. Yet here I was already contemplating when I'd be back in LA and if I could see her again.

Even if we stayed in touch, she was in the beginning stages of a divorce from the only man she'd ever been with until this weekend. The last thing she needed was to rebound directly into what? A long-distance relationship, at best?

Shaking off my thoughts of anything other than what we'd agreed on, I placed a Grubhub breakfast order to be delivered to my doorstep and checked my buzzing phone.

Shit. I'd forgotten all about my Zoom call with my producer. Sending him a quick response to give me a couple minutes, I went back inside. After feeding Callie, I grabbed my laptop and earbuds before sitting at my dining table.

Gary Radner came up on the screen. He was a seasoned veteran in the music industry and had produced my last three albums. "Did you oversleep, Deacon?"

"Something like that. How are you?"

"Good, good." He quirked his head to the side. "I thought you were in LA until Monday?"

"I'm sitting in my house right now. Why?"

"Huh. Guess it's because you normally don't seem this relaxed unless you're at home in Australia writing songs."

My demeanor was absolutely a product of my night with Andrea. "Yeah, maybe I look this way because I had an inspiration for a song this morning. Anyhow, I'm still on schedule to travel on Monday."

I went on to talk about timing and booked some recording studio dates four months from now. As I was about to wrap up the call, I glanced up, and my jaw dropped open. Because in walked Andrea, completely nude and shyly smiling.

"Uh, Gary. I need to go." With the vision in front of me, I was in a hurry to get off the call. Clicking the disconnect button, I slammed down the lid of the laptop and stood up only to see Andrea's eyes go large.

"Oh my God. Were you on video call?" She turned to flee, but not before I was able to grab her arm.

"I was, and now I'm not." My fingers traced a line from her shoulders down her bare arms. "My brave girl," I murmured before taking her lips.

Suddenly I stopped, a thought so poignant striking me that I had no choice but to act on it. Taking her hand, I pulled her to the bedroom, but instead of taking her in my arms, I grabbed my notebook and furiously scratched down the words "my brave girl" as the title of my next song.

Her confused expression had me explaining. "You've inspired me to write a song about you."

"Seriously?"

"It's the burden and the joy of being around a songwriter." Putting the pad down, I planted another kiss on her. "Hopefully you'll take it as the compliment it's meant to be."

"Only if I get to hear it someday."

"Deal. Although I have to preface the promise by saying only a fraction of the songs I write get cut on an album." Not everything was a hit song ready for radio.

She shrugged. "Might be more special if I'm the only person to ever hear it."

So many people out there in the world would have the opposite view, but not Andrea. She truly was special. "Come on, my brave, sexy girl, I want to introduce you to my steam shower and all of the delicious things I have planned for you in it."

Chapter Fifteen
ANDREA

It turned out that the prospect of wearing my revenge dress and showing up at the *City of Angels* wrap party with my head high and Deacon on my arm came with a big side of nausea. Rationally, I could admire the sexy black dress Portia had fitted to me like a glove this evening and my hair left long down my back with chunky, soft curls. I could praise myself for drawing the perfect Taylor Swift cat eyes with my black eyeliner.

But emotionally, I was a big ball of anxiety. My overriding thought as we arrived at the private club the studio had obtained for the party was that I didn't want to be here, period. Given the glorious way I'd started the day, both in Deacon's bed and his shower, I had to assume it would end with things moving downhill in a horrific manner.

I swallowed hard as I took Deacon's offered hand and stepped out of the back seat of the black SUV.

He looked incredibly handsome in black slacks and a dark sapphire button-up shirt. He kept the large lapels open enough to show part of his chest tattoo as well as an intricate silver chain. I'd never known a man who could pull off wearing jewelry—but rock-star chic presented sexy and edgy on Deacon.

He pulled me in close, inhaling at my ear, and whispered, "You are beautiful, Andrea. And your ex will taste regret over losing you the moment you walk in. Meanwhile, I'll be the proudest guy in the room, knowing you've done me the honor of bringing me as your date."

My smile was genuine. He'd certainly managed to dust off my self-confidence during the last twenty-four hours. Having him as a lover had been an incredible way to shed my insecurities, but more important was the way he made me feel like we were a team going into the party tonight, that he had my back.

What was crazy was I couldn't ever remember having felt that way with my ex. It had been the "Jeff show" for so long, with me cheering him on in the background, that I'd forgotten what it was like to be with someone who allowed me into the light too.

"Thank you. I went into this weekend thinking this fake dating thing might be crazy, but I'm glad you're here with me."

"That makes two of us." He bent down to press his lips to mine in a soft kiss, but it turned deeper in a hurry. When he pulled away, his intense gaze making me aware I wasn't the only one affected. The shouts of our names pulled us from our trance.

Right. Showtime. The paparazzi went nuts with us showing up together and kissing in public. Yet, I had no regrets. Why should I mind publicizing my affection and attraction since it was the most authentic part of this weekend?

He took my hand firmly in his and led me to where security was holding open the front door.

Once inside, one of the show runners walked up with her headset on and a big smile. "I'm so happy you both are here. Wow, you look amazing, Andrea, and well, Deacon, I'm such a big fan. My name is Lexi."

Deacon flashed what I'd call his stage smile and extended his hand. "Lovely to meet you, Lexi."

Lexi seemed like she wanted to never let go. I knew the feeling.

She finally released his hand and glanced over her shoulder, sighing. "Uh, Jeff and Paula are already here."

After Jeff's text message last night telling me he wanted to talk when he got to the house and several subsequent calls and irate voicemails about Deacon being at our house, I had no desire to be in the same room with him. I don't know where he got off being angry with me, but I refused to let anyone treat me that way, let alone someone who'd once professed to love me to his dying day.

Fixing a smile, I shrugged. "Thanks, Lexi. We knew he would be."

"Have you decided if you'll do your interview?" She appeared hopeful that I'd spill my guts in a one-on-one tonight. Anything for ratings.

"I haven't decided, but I doubt it'll happen during the party." Emotions were running high enough, and I wasn't sure I wanted to open up to the public about my marriage and everything that had gone wrong. Not that I owed any loyalty to Jeff, but it was awfully personal information to share.

My answer clearly disappointed her. "Okay, have a good time, okay?"

"Thanks."

"Shall we get some drinks?" Deacon suggested.

"That would be wonderful." We went to the bar.

A couple of the *City of Angels* cast members were gathered there, and their eyes went wide when they saw my date. Patrick, one of the other principals on the show and Jeff's frenemy, blurted out, "Holy shit," before grinning widely and chuckling.

He and Jeff had often butted heads over the last two seasons, both of their egos competing for airtime and the sanctimonious upper hand in the season. I imagined Patrick was enjoying this turn of events more than anyone else here.

While his date and another couple occupied Deacon with what I could only call fandemonium, Patrick clinked his martini glass against mine. "You having the balls to show up here tonight looking gorgeous in that dress is sweet enough. But bringing Deacon Miller as your date—who, by the way, looks, no offense, even hotter than you if I were to swing that way—takes the cake."

I couldn't help but laugh. Deacon was undoubtedly hot. "No offense taken."

"Please tell me you're returning next season? Would be nice to get to know you outside of Jeff."

"I haven't decided if I'll come back. But thanks for the support, Patrick." I'd found him harmless for the most part. Immature and hungry for camera time, but hindsight afforded me the ability to see Jeff had been the same way.

The next twenty minutes went about the same, conversing with various cast and crew while I paid no attention to Jeff, who was standing across the room talking with Paula, his obvious glare seldom leaving me or my date. He was dressed in black slacks and a white collared shirt which I'd normally say made him look handsome. But the yuck of finding out he'd cheated had altered the way I viewed him. As for Paula, she wore a short, sparkling dress, her long legs on display. She'd always been a pretty girl, but I'd yet to see her leave

Jeff's side during the party or act like she was having a good time.

I settled into an indifference toward the situation, surprised at how easy it was to ignore him. Ironically, this was the first party I could remember where I was actually connecting with others, probably because Jeff wasn't dominating the conversation or steering it toward what he wanted to talk about.

Here was Deacon, with a hundred times the public attention and a bona fide A-list star, but in contrast, he would generously turn the conversation toward the other person talking, or to me. He was gracious, charming, and genuine.

"I'm running to the ladies' room," I whispered into Deacon's ear and was surprised when he took the opportunity of my proximity to sneak a quick kiss.

"I'll order you another drink and be waiting."

It feels real. I wasn't surprised by the thought as I walked away from him. I only wished I could've kept it tamped down deep enough inside that I didn't actually think it and thus potentially ruin the perfect weekend.

Lest I forget, like Cinderella, this ball was over at the stroke of midnight. Then it was back to reality.

As I was doing my business in the stall, I heard the main door to the bathroom open. I didn't think anything of it until Jeff's voice rang out. "We need to talk, Andrea."

"For fuck's sake. I'm peeing."

"I'll wait."

The absurdity of the moment nearly caused me to giggle. After I was done, I straightened my dress, took a deep breath, and walked forward to the sink to wash my hands, completely disregarding his presence.

"What the hell are you wearing?"

In the mirror reflection I caught his gaze angrily raking

over my dress as though he had any right to the question. I refused to answer.

"You're not speaking to me now?"

"I'm not responding to your asshole questions, no."

"We need to talk," he repeated, causing me to arch a brow.

"Then you do the talking because I have nothing left to say to you."

He had the audacity to appear hurt. "This isn't you, babe."

The once familiar term of endearment turned my stomach. "Maybe it is now."

His entire face softened. "I've been thinking, and I want us to go to counseling to work on our relationship. My mom called and said that our pastor will counsel us. Maybe we go home to Kansas for a couple weeks, ya know."

Blink. Blink. He couldn't be serious. "You cheated on me with someone I considered a friend, and you're asking to go home and 'work on some things'?" There hadn't even been an apology, let alone any remorse.

"I still love you, Andrea. But you haven't exactly been supportive of my band or the bar, and—"

Oh, no, he didn't. "Don't you dare gaslight me and make excuses. I have been supportive in every single thing you've done. Even when it didn't make money." I'd been the breadwinner while he pursued his passions during our entire relationship.

He scrubbed a hand over his face. "I get to be a different person with Paula."

Hindsight was a kick in the ass considering Paula practically hero-worshipped him and fed his ego. "I'm sure you do. And the truth is I don't like that person you've become at all."

"I can change, I promise. Seeing you with Deacon is killing me."

Ah. Of course this was what was motivating his sudden hope for reconciliation. Like a kid who'd put down his favorite toy in favor of a new one, he'd been happy with the decision until the point he saw someone else pick it up.

Although I'd had no intention of releasing all of my pent-up resentment, he'd unleashed it. He had the nerve to think we'd simply go back to the way things had been because he was jealous of my trade-up?

"You threw away your integrity for a chance at fame. And when it came to choosing the person who loved you or this artificial life, you chose fame."

"It's not like it's been easy. I'm being crucified in the media currently. The bar has one-star reviews before it's opened."

"And I'm what? Supposed to feel sorry for you? You're a liar and a cheater, and what I've realized since you've been gone is I don't miss you. Because you're not the man I fell in love with, and I deserve better."

It was true. I no longer viewed him as my future or a man I wanted to be around and I certainly didn't miss him. Over the past few days, I'd started to realize I hadn't been happy in my marriage in quite awhile.

"What, you have a rock star pretend to be your date, and suddenly you're over me?"

"Wasn't anything pretend about the way she stayed with me last night," came Deacon's voice from the door.

Jeff's jaw clenched, his gaze ping-ponging between us. "This farce isn't going to last."

He wasn't wrong, but I wouldn't give him the satisfaction of admitting it.

Deacon chuckled, taking a casual pose against the frame

as only a sexy rock star could. "I suppose losing Andi would make any man bitter and grasping at straws."

Jeff's eyes bugged out, and he turned to me with accusation in his voice. "He calls you Andi?"

I'd never allowed even him to call me by that nickname, and it was clear how jealous he was in hearing it.

"Ready to go, Andi?" Deacon wasn't above making the dig twice. Although I didn't need the rescue, I appreciated it.

Jeff pivoted toward Deacon, bright red in the face. "You can see yourself out. I'm having a private conversation with my wife."

"Ex-wife. You should get used to saying it," I retorted. I was done with this and ready to get this man out of my life.

He practically snarled, "So this is how it's going to be? You thinking you can treat me like you're better than me just because you're fucking him? Fine. I'm going to make your life hell and take you to court over every single item in the house, including the fucking dog."

Deacon moved out of the doorway, allowing Jeff to storm past like the egotistical ass he was. I closed my eyes and refused to react to his threat. The problem was he'd already proven himself spiteful enough to carry through on it.

Deacon put his arms around me, rubbing my back. "I'm sorry. I shouldn't have goaded him. I'm sure you had it covered, but when I saw him walk back this direction, I couldn't leave you alone with him."

"It's just stuff." Material things could be replaced. "At the end of the day, I'll give him anything to keep Callie and be done."

Chapter Sixteen
DEACON

I'd never been a man of violence, but the anger I felt toward Jeff had me seeing red. It was all I could do not to punch him the hell out. But physical violence would only garner me an assault charge followed by a lawsuit.

"I'll give you whatever you need to settle with that prick."

She leaned back from our embrace, her eyes wide. "Meaning money?"

Jeff threatening to go after Andrea's dog was the last straw. I'd do or pay anything to ensure she didn't have to deal with his petty bullshit. Including buying him out.

"I can make an anonymous offer so generous on the house that he can't refuse. I would stipulate it come furnished and include you getting custody of Callie as a condition for the sale. Then you wouldn't have to deal with the coming battle."

From my first taste of success, people had come out of the woodwork to ask me for money. From high school classmates who sought investment capital for their latest ventures to cousins who felt entitled to share in my wealth because we shared a bloodline, I'd heard it all. My own father had thought I owed him even after he'd treated my mom like shit.

I was generous with those closest to me—I'd bought my mother a house—but as a rule I didn't offer money. Especially to those I barely knew.

But Andrea was the exception.

I took out my phone to fire off a text to my manager and make it happen, but her response was not one I'd expected.

"Absolutely not."

I glanced up from the text I was composing. "What? Why not?"

She was about to tell me, but a woman came into the restroom. Her face expressed shock at the both of us.

I threw her a smile. "We were just leaving."

Taking Andi's hand, I led her down the hall toward the back exit so we could be alone. Inhaling deeply, I realized I was coming across as controlling.

"I want to help. Please let me." When was the last time I'd been desperate to offer money, and someone wouldn't accept? I wasn't sure it had ever happened.

She took both my hands in hers. "And I appreciate it more than I could ever say, but I could never accept money from you or anyone else. I need to do this on my own. Or at least with the help of the attorney I hired. What we really need to do is sell everything, so Jeff can pay me back some of the money he owes me."

Hold up. "He borrowed money from you?"

"He borrowed against the equity in the house. Since that's considered marital funds, he doesn't necessarily owe me money."

"What did he do with the money?"

"He invested in a bar in Hollywood."

"He's an owner?" An idea started to take root.

"He and three other partners went in on it. He has a ten percent stake."

"But if the equity in the house belongs to both of you, wouldn't the investment in the bar belong to you too? We're in a community property state. Unless you signed something saying it was only his?"

Her eyes went wide before her smile did. "I didn't sign anything of the sort. Which means I have part of the stake in the bar too. Holy shit, Deac. This could be it. The leverage I need to ensure he doesn't fight me over Callie."

I loved the way she called me Deac. And I admired how she wasn't letting Jeff's threats overwhelm her. Instead, she seemed ready to meet them with her own demands. The only thing that concerned me was that a good shark attorney would already have pointed out to her the leverage she had.

"You need a better divorce lawyer. I know someone who's one of the best out there. His name is Lawrence Gerson." He'd represented my mom during her divorce from my father ten years ago and had ensured the bastard didn't get anything more than he deserved. "Let me contact him for you?"

"If the favor is to make the call, then yes, but I'll be the one paying him."

"Absolutely." If I had to supplement his fee, I would do so and deal with her anger later if she found out. "I'll text him right now."

I typed a quick text, asking if Lawrence was available to take a new case. Unbeknownst to Andrea, I added a second message that I'd call him tomorrow with some additional details, namely the reasonable rate I wanted him to present to her.

We returned to the main room in time to see Jeff arguing with a blonde in the corner. I assumed this was his mistress,

Paula. The woman stomped off with him quickly following, the whole altercation bringing all eyes upon the two of them.

Andrea expelled a long breath. "God, it feels good to have his tantrums be someone else's problem tonight. Meanwhile —" She took my hand and smiled up at me. "I get to look forward to my evening."

The wave of possessiveness that took hold of me was something I'd never experienced before. Not only did I want to help and protect her, but I found myself reluctant to let her go. "How much longer are you contractually required to be here?"

She held my wrist and glanced at my watch. "Half an hour. And that might be just enough time to do an interview."

"You're sure it's what you want?" My gaze studied her face.

"Yes. I was hesitant to share personal details, but considering the way Jeff is behaving, I'm ready to reveal my side of the story."

Ten minutes later, the two producers of the show along with a filming crew led us into the back room to conduct the interview. I'd asked if she wanted to be alone, but she'd allowed me to stay in the room. The first few questions probed for her feelings about the affair.

But the topic of conversation shifted quickly. "Regarding Deacon Miller as your date tonight, where do you think your future stands with him?"

I should've anticipated the interviewer would be curious about us. My breath held as I watched her glance over to me, her cheeks turning pink.

"Deacon and I have started an incredible friendship. He's made me realize how nice it feels to be treated well. And once you've adopted a new standard, you don't go back."

"Jeff mentioned in his interview you weren't supportive of him. What do you say to that?"

"In this world, there are people who give, and there are people who take. Jeff has taken for so long that he doesn't recognize what it is to give, or what happens when the people he's taken from have nothing more to give. He continues to be a taker. Tonight he went so far as to threaten to take my dog when I wouldn't agree to give him another chance. The taking has gotten downright petty. He's affixed Post-it notes with his name on them to all the items he wants in the house."

She continued talking, discussing their fertility struggles and how she'd lost the man she'd once known. I was proud of her for not holding anything back.

My brave girl.

The interviewer was also a producer and seemed genuinely to care for Andrea. Throughout, his tone had been kind.

Then came the final question. "Will you return next year to the show?"

I could practically hear Ollie's voice and hoped she'd be cautious. If she said no, the producers of the show might not have an incentive to share her side. "I don't know yet, Brett. There's a lot to figure out."

"If you don't return, do you have anything to say to your fans?"

"I'd tell them thank you for your support. I'd also say to you and the rest of the crew that I appreciate how kind everyone has been to me. This show and being on it was way out of my comfort zone, but you all made it easier."

She was smart to compliment the crew and equally shrewd to avoid committing to returning. I wasn't sure when this would air, but it was important not to burn bridges.

Afterward, Andi pasted on a smile while she said her

goodbyes, but it was obvious from the way she gripped my hand that she was emotionally drained. I'd hoped to get her outside and into the waiting car, but Paula came out of nowhere, intercepting us in the entryway.

"Hi, Andrea. Can I have a word?" She licked her lips, appearing nervous. "Please."

For a moment, I thought Andi might deny her the opportunity, but she sighed. "You have two minutes."

"Do you want me to step away?" I wanted to support her but would respect her potential need for privacy.

She offered me a lopsided smile. "No, you can stay."

The blonde flicked her gaze to me before centering her focus on Andi. Tears were already forming in her eyes. "I wanted to say I'm sorry. I didn't mean—" She took a gulp of air. "I didn't mean to hurt you especially when you were a good friend to me."

"What did you think would happen when you slept with my husband?"

Paula visibly flinched and clearly had no good answer to the question. Meanwhile, I was reminded just how recent and raw this all was for Andrea. Although we might be having an incredible weekend together, she was still grieving her marriage.

Paula inhaled sharply, tears now falling. "He said you were getting divorced, and I believed him."

Of course he'd fed her a false narrative. A tale as old as time.

But Andrea wasn't letting her off the hook. "And yet you were hanging out with us both, so you had to know that wasn't true. You chose to ignore the signs all around you and believe the lies. And Jeff continues to lie because I can guarantee he didn't tell you that thirty minutes ago he asked me to go to counseling and work on staying together."

Paula's face blanched.

Meanwhile Andi's tone wasn't gloating or competitive, but rather she sounded resigned. "My days of looking out for you or giving you advice are over, Paula. You can choose to continue to believe him or not. It's no longer my business."

"Will you accept my apology?"

She didn't hesitate. "While I appreciate your apology, I don't accept it. Because there are some things which aren't forgivable, and sleeping with a married man while befriending his wife is in that category. But I do wish you well."

Again, she wasn't being cruel. Merely honest. And I was happy to see her standing up for herself.

Paula's shoulders slumped, the words clearly not what she'd wanted to hear. "I understand."

Andi turned to me. "I'm ready to go."

I kept my arm around her as I led her out to the waiting SUV, unsure who more needed her close, me or her. "I'm so proud of you."

"Thanks. Did you think I was too hard on her?"

The fact she worried about it testified to her character.

"You were more than fair. Betrayal is not something you need to forgive."

"No, I don't need to absolve them of anything in order to move on."

Once in the back seat, I lifted her legs up onto my lap and removed one shoe at a time. It was a pleasure to hear her sigh of relief.

"What does moving on look like? Say five years from now?" I was curious to find out how Andrea saw her future.

"I hope to have a family. Maybe open my own business and do freelance website design, and I don't know, there's that animal sanctuary idea even if it's a couple cats and dogs, and maybe one mini cow to start."

Her long-term plan shouldn't have surprised me, but hearing her talk about a future that wouldn't include me left me feeling out of sorts.

The emotion was ridiculous. Here she was, navigating a divorce and picking up the pieces of her life. The last thing she needed was to jump into another relationship. Not that I knew what that would be like. We'd enjoy the rest of the weekend and say our goodbyes, just as we'd agreed.

"If you don't have any plans tomorrow, I thought we could hang out at my place? I don't leave until Monday morning."

She smiled. "I don't have any plans, and I wouldn't mind avoiding my house, but don't you have things to do before you leave? More Zoom calls where you don't need a—" She paused, flicking her gaze to the driver who was staring straight ahead. "A houseguest interrupting?"

The way she omitted the naked part made me chuckle. "I can't think of a better interruption. And aside from a few phone calls, I don't have a thing planned."

Chapter Seventeen
ANDREA

Who could possibly say no to spending more time with Deacon? Especially when he was rubbing my feet in the back of an SUV. Yet there was the small voice warning that I was in over my head and shouldn't go and do something stupid like fall for the man. He was most certainly leaving town, while I'd be left sitting here in reality.

The same voice told me it might already be too late. This may have started as a weekend of pretend, but it was turning out to be the best two days of my life.

Tonight had been cathartic. I'd finally been strong enough to share my true feelings with Jeff, and then the world, and even with Paula.

Jeff had wanted our lives on reality television, and now he had it. The good, bad, and now the ugly. I had no doubt he'd be furious once the interview aired, but I no longer cared. I was ready to move on. I was also ready to eat, having not done so since lunch.

"You hungry?"

He grinned. "Starving."

It was close to nine o'clock, but I had an idea. "I know the perfect place." I directed the driver to the best taco truck stand in LA. When we arrived, I was amused to see Deacon bring out my slippers which he'd thoughtfully stowed in the car for me.

We'd just ordered when Deacon's phone rang. "Ah, it's my attorney friend. How's it going, Lawrence?"

Deacon listened for a bit before looking at me. "Yeah, let me ask her. You okay with meeting Lawrence tomorrow?"

"Of course." So much for spending the day with Deacon. But the financial situation regarding my divorce was too important to put off.

Once we received our order, which included two fish tacos Deacon obtained for the driver, I played photographer, snapping phone pictures of him and the crew who manned the truck and a couple fellow customers who also wanted pictures with him. He was friendly to everyone, and I found myself once again wishing there wasn't a countdown on our time together.

Back at Deacon's house, Callie greeted us at the front door, clearly anxious to have me home.

Despite his designer clothes, he crouched down to pet her. "Come on, pretty girl, let's go outside." He led her down the hall and let her out the sliding back door after turning on the lights so she could see the grass.

"I should go out and clean up after her." I grabbed a bag from her leash.

"I'll do it in the morning. Come out and see this though."

I took his hand, and he led me out back. "Wow. How did I miss this last night?" The view from his backyard of the LA cityscape was gorgeous.

He chuckled, wrapping his arms around me from the back

and nuzzling my neck. "Probably because I had you distracted."

"Mm, it was a lovely distraction." Turning in his arms, I marveled at how quickly I'd become comfortable enough to reach up and kiss him. My affectionate action seemed like the most natural thing in the world.

If this was my last night with him, I mused, then I'd make it count.

Chapter Eighteen
DEACON

I'd always been an early riser, but on Sunday morning I got up extra early, fighting a restlessness I couldn't seem to shake. I then did what I always did if anxiety crept up—I sweated it out.

Although my LA house didn't have the full gym facility my Australia home boasted, it did have a treadmill and a set of weights in one of the spare bedrooms. After running five miles and lifting with purpose, I sat on the bench, finally ready to be honest about the reason for my agitation.

I'd caught feelings for the woman currently in my bed. It made no sense given our timeframe. Perhaps the sensation was a side effect of us faking it. Grabbing my iPad, I queued up the first season of *City of Angels,* desperate to discover what it was that had me fascinated.

Two episodes in, I turned it off, pissed off at her selfish ex and jealous of how in love and supportive of him she'd been. Determined to ensure Andrea wasn't screwed over by the prick, I dialed Lawrence, aware he was also an early riser.

"You know I'd only answer the phone for you at six something in the morning."

"Appreciate it. I wanted to talk to you before you meet with Andrea later today."

"And you're whispering because she's asleep beside you?"

What I both admired and found annoying about Lawrence was his candor. "She's in the other room." I proceeded to explain how I wanted to supplement his rate and for him to bill me directly.

He let out a long sigh. "I don't keep secrets from my clients. Why not tell her that you're footing the bill?"

"Because she won't take the money. And without a shark, her ex will get more than he deserves." I described the way Jeff had used their home equity to fund his bar.

"How about instead of billing you the difference, you do me a big favor?"

"Name it." I preferred this idea.

"My daughter and her friends are huge fans. Sing a couple songs at her birthday party in October."

My manager would have a complete fit over me agreeing to do a kid's birthday party, but I didn't care. "Consider it done. Send me the date, and we'll make it happen."

"If your girlfriend agrees to my representation, then be confident I'll go for the jugular."

I didn't bother to correct his assumption about Andrea being my girlfriend. "Good."

After hanging up, I took a quick shower and made breakfast, intending to bring it to her in bed. But she puttered out to the kitchen before I'd finished, wearing my robe and looking absolutely adorable with her messy bun and sleepy eyes. How easy was it to imagine more mornings like this?

"Hi, beautiful. Did I wake you?"

"Mm, the smell of bacon did." She let Callie outside

before heading over to nip a piece I'd placed on a paper towel.

"Guess I won't ever make you choose between me and bacon."

She laughed, licking her lips and going in for a kiss. "Smart man. Did you sleep all right?"

"I get anxious before I take time off to write." It wasn't a complete lie.

She let Callie back in and gave her a scoop of food. "Anxious in what way?"

I was always careful what I shared regarding my creative process because I didn't want to sound ungrateful. "I'm thankful for the success I've achieved, but every time I go into the studio, I fear my next effort won't be as good as the other albums."

"I suppose it would be tough to keep raising the bar, especially when it's so high already. Of all the songs you've written, which is your favorite?"

Leave it to her to make it easy to talk to her. We spent the rest of the morning in casual banter before I drove her to a nondescript office building where Lawrence rented space. Given how often he worked for high-profile clients, he rotated office locations every year so as to make it less obvious who might be seeking him out. I hoped we'd get lucky and be able to avoid the paparazzi.

"Thanks for driving me," she said, appearing nervous in the passenger seat.

"Happy to. I have an appointment with my record label, but it won't take long."

I'd just finished up the meeting and was shooting the shit with people on my team when my phone buzzed. I smiled when I saw it was a text from Andrea, but it dropped when I actually read it.

Shit. She was on her way to confront her ex.

"I have to go."

Chapter Nineteen

ANDREA

Lawrence was a handsome, forty-something-year-old man with wisps of gray in his black hair that made him look both distinguished and debonair.

It was immediately clear he intended to be aggressive in his approach. "My job is to get you what is fair, and I will stop at nothing to make sure that happens. I'm quick, I'm relentless, and I guarantee once Jeff's attorney finds out who is now representing you, he will be more amenable to agreeing to an out-of-court settlement."

A week ago I would've hesitated in engaging an attorney who was out for blood, but that was before Jeff had threatened to take my dog. Now the gloves were off.

"I'm on board with your plans, but we should discuss price."

He sat back in his chair to regard me. "I'll be honest. Deacon discussed the rate with me and seemed to think I'd be out of your range. So he offered to do me a big favor in exchange for me giving you the same rate you're paying your present attorney."

"What favor?" The last thing I wanted was Deacon taking on my debt.

"He agreed to sing at my daughter's birthday party, and if you say no, I guarantee she and her friends will never forgive you."

I smiled. Singing at a birthday party sounded harmless enough. "What is your typical rate?"

"Twelve hundred an hour."

Holy shit. I was paying four hundred and fifty and thought that was high.

"My daughter is twelve, and sometimes I'm an absentee father given the hours I work, so believe me when I say the trade is well worth it to me. Plus I'm intrigued."

"Intrigued how?"

"Deacon isn't a guy who goes out on a limb for anyone, which means you must be special. Why don't you tell me about Jeff and how your finances are situated."

It took thirty minutes to detail out everything. Lawrence took notes the whole while. "Who are the other partners in the bar?"

When I gave him the names, his brows rose. "One of them is a reputable financier who won't want his deal to get messy. When does the bar open for business?"

"Their grand opening is next month. Jeff is there every day getting things together."

"I think it's time to meet him on his own turf."

Turned out my new attorney had a flair for the dramatic, as illustrated by his plan. If going along with his scheme meant I could settle this divorce quickly and get custody of my dog, then I was happy to play my part.

"You ready?" He pulled his fancy Mercedes in front of the new bar.

"You bet I am."

I was thankful I'd thrown a silk top into the bag I'd brought with me to Deacon's house along with the high heels I'd worn to the wedding. At the time, it had been a whim on the off chance I might need to dress up. Now they added a touch of elegance to the jeans I had on. I'd take any edge to ease my nerves.

But what worked the best at easing my nerves was thinking back to my incredible morning with Deacon. He'd helped me regain my confidence, and I wasn't about to let anyone, especially not my soon-to-be ex-husband, steal it from me ever again.

Lawrence flashed me a reassuring smile. In his expensive suit and shoes, an outfit that probably cost more than my mortgage payment, he appeared every bit the high-priced lawyer. "You sure you're okay going in there alone?"

Although he could ethically represent me in legal matters, it was murky for him to assist me in the coming confrontation. Therefore, he'd agreed to wait outside.

But before I could beard the lion in his den, a familiar, exotic car drove up. Deacon. He was the last person I'd expected to see here.

He got out of the car looking anxious.

"What are you doing here?" I asked.

"I wanted to be here for you in case you needed me." He turned to shake Lawrence's hand. "Are you going in there with her?"

Looking amused, Lawrence shook his head. "I really can't. But you could."

It was tempting to bring Deacon along, but this was something I needed to do on my own. Not only did I want to continue my journey of taking back control, but he would be on a plane come tomorrow. I couldn't get used to having him in my corner.

"Thanks, but I need to handle this one by myself."

He appeared disappointed but nodded. "Of course."

I hadn't been to the bar since they'd signed the lease, so it was strange to walk in and see it built out with the space taking shape. But I experienced no emotional reaction to seeing Jeff's dream come to life. Instead, to my relief, I was officially detached from it all.

I didn't see anyone inside until I reached the back. There, several men in suits were gathered around a table studying blueprints and swatches with different color palettes.

All gazes swung to me. Jeff's eyes went wide. "What the hell are you doing here, Andrea?"

Oh shit. I hadn't expected such a large audience. I hoped the shake stayed out of my voice. "Given I'm part owner now, I thought I'd drop in to take a peek."

An older gentleman with silver hair and beard squinted. I recognized him as being one of the other investors. "What is she talking about, Jeff?"

Pasting on a smile, I drew in a deep breath to steady myself. "Oh, he didn't tell you? Guess it must've slipped his mind. His investment money came from refinancing our home, and since that is jointly owned, it means half of the hundred thousand he put up is my money, so I'm a five percent owner. Of course, after the divorce, I can sell my shares to anyone I choose."

The three other men at the table started arguing. Jeff, looking irate, took my elbow to lead me to the side. "You come in here when I'm meeting with the other owners? To what, embarrass me?"

It hadn't been my intention, but if it put more pressure on him, perhaps it was a good thing. "This is what you asked for when you threatened to fight over every single thing, including my dog. So let's fight."

He appeared a combination of shocked and furious. "This isn't you."

"You keep saying that to me, and I agree that it didn't use to be me. But thanks to you dropping a grenade into our marriage and then having the nerve to treat me as if I deserved the affair with your callous attitude, this is what you get. A woman who isn't about to lie down and take it."

"The bar is my dream." He used the cajoling tone which had always gotten him his way. But not this time.

"Then I suggest you agree to sell the house, pay me back the hundred thousand out of the sale, not fight me on Callie, and be overly generous regarding the furniture and other items I request."

"Paula and I are in a big fight." He actually had the nerve to sound hurt. What did he think I would do—comfort him?

"I don't care." I really didn't. Maybe he actually loved her, maybe he didn't. Neither alternative made a difference to me. The man in front of me had never put me or our marriage first. Hadn't honored his vows. Hadn't kept his promises. And I deserved better.

"You and Deacon are for real, huh?"

Real at least until he left tomorrow morning. "None of your business. This is about the bar, the house, and Callie. Nothing else. I want this settled as quickly as possible. You won't win in court, and you certainly won't win in the public eye."

He heaved a sigh as he caught the eye of his investors. "Shit. Fine. If you agree not to fight me on the bar investment, then I'll give you what you want with the house and the dog."

"I'll have my lawyer draw up the division of assets. In the meantime, I'll be taking residence in the home. I expect you to move your things out in the next two weeks and the house to be listed in the next thirty days."

He pinched the bridge of his nose. "Fine."

"Goodbye, Jeff."

"Wait."

I paused, wondering what parting words he had. Would he say he was sorry? Reflect on over a decade of love lost? "What is it?"

But he capped off our relationship by acting like the flaming asshole he'd become. "I definitely want my car and all of my frequent flier miles."

He made it so easy to walk away for good. "I'm sure both can be arranged."

Walking out of the bar, it felt as if a weight had been lifted. Both Deacon and Lawrence were waiting for me outside.

Chapter Twenty

DEACON

I was so freaking proud of Andrea I was nearly bursting with it. And although I selfishly would've loved to have been inside to see the smugness wiped from Jeff's face, I knew it was something she'd needed to do on her own.

Equally as selfish, I wished I could have had her all to myself for the remainder of the day, but watching her smile and laugh with Lawrence and Ollie as we all met for lunch and champagne made the sacrifice of time worthwhile.

As we arrived back at my house in the afternoon, I could feel the remaining hours of the weekend slipping away. Taking her into my arms in the middle of my living room, I intended to spend the next few hours with her naked in my bed, in my shower, and wherever else the mood struck us.

But as soon as I started kissing her, my gate bell rang. I had every intention of ignoring it.

"What's that sound?" Andi asked.

"Someone who is trying to suck time away from us." It couldn't be anyone I actually wanted to see because they would've texted or called first.

"Don't you want to find out who it is?"

I should've said no, but I made the mistake of thinking I could deal with it quickly and thus end Andrea's distraction. I took out my phone and brought up the app for the gate. "Hello?"

"Hi, it's Nina."

My wide eyes met Andrea's. "She should be on her honeymoon, for Christ's sake," I grumbled.

"Are you going to let her in?"

The bell rang again, then again. "I could have security remove her."

Andrea's face softened. "But that could end up in the tabloids, and probably upset Bryce and your mom."

She wasn't wrong about this being a potential mess. Better to simply meet this head-on. "You're right."

"Do you want me to give you two privacy?"

"No, I'd rather you stay." Not because I wanted to sell a fake relationship any longer, but because I honestly wanted Andrea by my side.

"Then I'll stay."

I pressed the button to open the gate and waited for her to drive up, physically flinching when the knock came. Dread wasn't a strong enough word.

After I opened the door, Nina walked in as if she owned the place, only stopping in my living room when Callie puttered in to check out the houseguest. "Whose dog is that?"

Andrea came in from the kitchen. "Callie is my dog. Nice to see you again, Nina."

Andi's kind greeting was next-level high road. But she was the only one driving it as Nina instantly showed her annoyance by her presence. "I need to speak with Deacon alone."

"Whatever you have to say you can say in front of Andi.

Especially since you have ten minutes before we need to get back to our plans."

She huffed before promptly bursting into tears, but I wasn't dealing with her manipulative nonsense.

I took a seat on the sofa, with Andi beside me. Words could not describe how badly I wanted to spend time with her instead of dealing with my ex.

Nina immediately stopped the waterworks as soon as it was clear she wouldn't get her way.

"What do you want?" I was out of patience.

She took a seat on one of the chairs. "Bryce and I fought on the honeymoon. It isn't going to work between us."

"Why would you come here?"

"Because I thought—I was hoping..."

I'd tried being nice. I'd tried being honest. Now it was time to be blunt. "Bryce is the best thing to ever happen to you. You should've seen the look on his face when you were walking down the aisle. But you didn't see because you were too busy looking at me. He loves you."

She dabbed at her eyes. "Did you ever love me?"

"No. And you are damn lucky to have someone love you the way Bryce does. But this—" I motioned between us. "Will never happen. Ever."

"Are you really taking her to Australia with you?" Her gaze flicked to Andrea beside me.

I gripped Andi's hand hoping she didn't mind perpetuating the lie. "Yes, she's joining me in a few weeks, and you need to go home to your husband, Nina."

She seemed to realize this was the end of whatever fantasy she'd been perpetuating. "You won't tell him I was here?"

"I won't lie. If he asks, I can tell him you came here for advice. But no more bullshit. This is it."

She nodded, real tears running down her face. "I understand."

When I stood up to see her out, she went in for the hug. Although it went against every instinct for me to give it to her, I went along with it, hoping it would help provide whatever closure she was searching for. Once she left, I shut the door and leaned against it, relieved she was gone.

"How are you?" Andrea asked, concern etched on her beautiful face.

"Better now that she's gone." Gripping the back of my neck, I addressed the possible elephant in the room. "Sorry I lied about you joining me in Australia."

Her smile was soft. "Not any different than the way I lied to Jeff about us being an item. It's fine."

I blew out the breath I'd been holding over her getting the wrong idea; thankful we were still on the same page about this being one weekend only.

I pulled her into my arms. "Now that we've completed our gauntlet of exes, and I'm about to turn off both of our phones, how would you like to spend the rest of our time together?"

She grinned. "Oh, I have some ideas."

Chapter Twenty-One
ANDREA

The sound of Deacon's alarm going off in the morning was akin to having cold water thrown on us.

Our one weekend together was officially over.

He kissed my forehead before heaving himself out of the bed and heading directly into the shower. Although I could've joined him, the state of my emotions had me staying where it was safe.

As if Callie sensed my mood, she came over to put her head on my leg.

"I know, girl. Come on." I dressed quickly in sweats and took her outside to the backyard to do her business. Taking out my phone, I ordered an Uber to arrive in thirty minutes.

"You could've stayed in bed longer," Deacon remarked, walking out the sliding glass door. He was wearing nothing but a low-slung pair of jeans.

Dear Universe, just make it even harder for me to leave, why don't you?

"I'm sure you need to pack and get to the airport. Plus, I should get home as I have to work today." I'd taken Friday off and had a lot to do to catch up as there was a project due in a few days' time. But work was actually an excuse to get out of here before my feelings about never seeing him again erupted into tears.

"I can make you breakfast. Drive you home."

It was tempting to prolong the inevitable, but saying goodbye in a car in front of my house with the paparazzi staked out to get a picture of the intimate moment was the last thing I wanted. "Thanks. But I arranged a car to pick me up. It should be here in half an hour."

He stepped back, shoving his hands in his pockets. "Right. Okay. I'll let you get ready."

I packed up my bags quickly, with Deacon nowhere to be seen. I had everything ready to go by the front door when he came walking toward me. Fully dressed now, he presented an unreadable face.

He'd been clear regarding our mutual expectations for the weekend, and I had no regrets in spending it with him. There'd been enough drama from our exes over the last few days that I was sure he was anxious to get to the other side of the world, and I didn't begrudge him his well-earned escape.

A few weeks from now, Deacon would be deep in his writing cave, the press about us would die down, and I'd hopefully be looking at an amenable divorce agreement in the rearview mirror, just waiting for the judge to sign off. Although I was anxious about my future, I was also looking forward to having the independence to make my own decisions for the first time in years.

The buzz at the gate announced the Uber driver had arrived. Deacon pulled up the video and sighed as he hit the button to let the driver in.

"Here, I'll help you load up." He grabbed Callie's bed and my suitcase, taking them out to the SUV.

When the driver got out to help him, Deacon slipped him a bill. Judging from the driver's face, it had been a big one. "Please help Ms. Foreman unload when you get to her home."

"Absolutely, sir. Thank you."

I turned to hug him one more time, but squeaked when he took my hand and pulled me backward.

"Give us two minutes," Deacon told him.

Once we were back inside of his house, he shut the door and slammed his lips to mine, completely devouring and devastating me with our last kiss. When he pulled away, we were both panting heavily. Laying his forehead against mine, he sighed. "I needed our goodbye to be private."

I ran my hands over his back, memorizing his warmth and muscular build. "I'm glad you did."

Taking a set of keys from his pocket, he put them in my hand.

"What are these?"

"Keys to this place if ever you need an escape. And before you say no, understand that I wouldn't offer these to just anyone. I trust you, and it would make me feel better to know you have a refuge if you need it. I'll text you the alarm and gate codes."

Tears welled up in my eyes. I didn't think I'd ever use his house, but his thoughtfulness and generosity overwhelmed me. "It means a lot to me. This entire weekend has changed my life at a time I desperately needed it. Thank you for everything."

"Promise you'll reach out if you have any trouble with Jeff or your attorney or anything else?"

"Yeah, I promise."

My voice was thick with emotion, and I needed to leave before it boiled over into tears.

Chapter Twenty-Two

DEACON

I binged both seasons of *City of Angels* on my way to Sydney, and like a pathetic stalker, I rewound the scenes with Andrea time and time again. She was beautiful. She was funny. She was down to earth.

But her bright light dulled during season two as Jeff put her through the wringer by selfishly spending more time with his band and co-stars than with her.

It was tough to witness how she'd put him first, and he'd tromped all over her sacrifice.

It had been on the tip of my tongue to ask her to come to Australia. But to what end? I'd been clear my retreat was the most special place on earth to me and I didn't invite people there. She and I had known each other for one weekend, so bringing her into my private sanctum would be a hell of a leap. Yet here I was, not even a full day away, and I was already missing her.

What was she doing right now? Would she use the keys and codes I'd sent her to stay in my LA house? My motive had been generosity, but I'd also felt desperate to keep a connection with her.

Turning my iPad off, I settled my seat into a reclining position on my private jet, intending to fall asleep. But instead all I could think about were shy smiles and sweet kisses. Giving up on sleep, I took out my notepad to write down those thoughts.

I was off to a good start with my songwriting, or so I thought. But two weeks later, it was clear my first ever case of writer's block had hit. I tried walking on the beach, working out to the point of exhaustion, and sitting with my guitar for hours. But nothing came.

Isolation used to be the way I recharged. But these last couple of weeks my solitude had instead felt like a prison.

It was tempting to text Andrea, but I was sure she was busy. I'd received nothing more than a one-word "thanks" when I'd sent her my gate and house codes.

FaceTiming my mom, I was happy when she answered on the first ring. "Hi, honey, how's life down under?"

"Okay. How are things with you?"

She made small talk before eyeing me the way only a mom could. "You don't look rested."

I sighed. "I'm not."

"Have you spoken with Andrea?"

"No."

She opened her mouth but then closed it.

"If you have something to say, please say it."

"Okay. I thought you two looked good together."

"But...she's going through a divorce and is in no position to start a new relationship so soon. Is that the part you were about to add?"

She chuckled. "That would be hypocritical given I met Rob while I was going through my divorce from your father. My concern is how you didn't seem to be doing anything about it."

I was stuck on the first part, however. How was this the first time I was hearing this? "Wait. You met Rob while going through your divorce from Dad?"

"We weren't exactly advertising our relationship to everyone. Honestly, I thought perhaps it was just one of those rebound things. I wasn't sure I wanted to jump right into another relationship."

"But you did. Why?"

"Because after a shitty first marriage, where the only good thing that came out of it was you, I realized I deserved a second chance at love. Why should I give that up because the timing wasn't in line with other people's expectations?" She paused. "Does she have a good attorney?"

"She has Lawrence Gerson."

"Then she's in good hands. You footing the bill?" my mom asked out of curiosity, not judgment.

"I offered, but she wouldn't hear of it."

"Another reason to like her. By the way, you failed to mention Nina came by your house after ditching her honeymoon early."

"I didn't tell you how she tricked me into seeing her before the wedding either. Both times I made it clear she should concentrate on her marriage."

She sighed. "Bryce said they were working on things. I wish he'd realize he deserves better."

"Me too. I miss Andrea."

My mom's eyes went wide at my unexpected admission. "Then why didn't you ask her to spend some time with you? You could have asked her to come visit you."

"You know how I feel about this place."

"Why are you putting so much pressure on this, sweetheart? You want to spend more time with her, and if that time happens to be in Australia, so what? It doesn't need to mean you've fast-forwarded twenty steps in the relationship. It can simply mean you want to get to know each other better. What I'm trying to say is you're placing a bigger importance than needs to be there on who gains entry to your house."

She was right. I was considering an invitation to Australia a gating item into a serious relationship, but it could be much simpler.

The conversation with my mother made me want to call Andrea, but before I did, I called Ollie to find out what she was up to.

"Hey, my good lad, how is the writing going?"

"It's, uh, been okay." If I told him it was dismal, he'd be concerned. The burning question on my mind was, "How's Andrea?"

"You could ask her yourself, you know."

"I'm not sure if she wants to hear from me." I hated the insecurity in my voice. But considering I hadn't heard from her, it was possible she wasn't missing me at all.

His chuckle was unexpected.

"You're laughing?"

"When something is absurd, then yes, yes I am."

"What's absurd?"

"Why are you calling me about Andrea? The truth."

I didn't hesitate. "Because I miss her. And before you say we only had the one weekend together—"

"Not at all what I was about to say. Instead, I'll tell you to pull your head out of your arse and tell her those exact words."

"I wasn't sure how to invite her here without it being a big deal, and putting pressure on both of us. Is she all right?"

"Yes, she's fine. Jeff moved out, and the house goes on the market in another couple days. The lawyer you recommended doesn't waste time. They have completed the mediation and divided the assets. It'll take six months for the judge to sign off, but it should be smooth sailing from here."

"Is her ex being fair?"

"She seems to think so, for the most part. Call her, Deacon."

"Yeah. Actually I have a better idea. Mind helping?"

"Thought you'd never ask."

Chapter Twenty-Three
ANDREA

I walked behind the real estate agent as she toured my house and took notes for the listing. I imagined all of my hard work in designing it would be summarized to something clinical like "newly remodeled kitchen with granite countertops and chef-grade appliances."

Jeff had moved out a week ago. I was thankful, but once he'd signed off on the division of assets, taking his car and frequent flier miles with him, he'd checked out of the process altogether, leaving all the logistics of the situation to me.

Last I'd heard he was overseas filming some competition show. The tabloids reported that he and Paula had broken up.

I didn't care. And it felt so freeing I no longer had to.

Switching my attention to what the agent was saying, I was surprised to hear she'd be ready to put it on the market the day after tomorrow.

"I will only accept private showings, but those will go better if you could go stay somewhere else with your dog. That way the bowls and beds are picked up, and things stay neat and tidy."

She was right. It made sense to move out temporarily

while they showed the house. I'd already boxed up a number of things and moved them to storage in order to keep the surfaces clean.

My thoughts drifted to the keys to his house that Deacon had left me. I hadn't intended to use them, but I found myself missing the connection we'd shared and wanting an excuse to be close to him, even if the only way of doing so was by staying in his house for a few days until I could make other dog-friendly accommodations.

I wondered, not for the first time, how he was doing. Aside from texting me his gate and house codes on the first day, he hadn't communicated with me. Then again, it wasn't like I'd reached out either. Maybe staying in his house would give me an excuse to start the conversation. After all, we were friends, and friends reached out.

Turning to the agent, I asked, "How long do you think it'll take to get an offer?"

She smiled confidently. "In this hot market, I expect to have multiple offers within a week."

"All right." Might as well get used to living elsewhere since the place wouldn't be mine much longer.

Selling this house was like closing a chapter of a book I no longer wanted to read. The question, of course, was which book I would pick up next. Perhaps I'd take a vacation. Find my own oasis to recharge and plan my future. The thought of getting out of LA and spending time off-grid held a lot of appeal.

I was quiet and deep in thought the next morning with Ollie in the passenger seat and my beloved dog in the back seat of my new Honda. I'd traded in my luxury car for something much more practical a few days ago and couldn't be happier with it. Meanwhile, Ollie had been nice enough to accompany me over to Deacon's house today and help with my suitcases. He'd even brought some travel books for inspiration.

"I texted Deacon about staying here, but he didn't answer." It felt strange to just show up without letting him know, but in reality I hoped this act would provide an excuse for us to start talking again.

Ollie smiled. "I'm sure he's deep in his writing cave and just hasn't had time to respond yet. He'll be happy to hear you're using his house."

I hoped he was right.

I pulled in front of Deacon's gate and typed in the code wishing he would've responded to my text so I didn't feel like I was imposing.

Once I parked at the top of the driveway, I got out of the car on shaky legs, a host of memories flooding back.

Ollie got out with Callie on her leash. "I'll walk her around and grab some stuff if you want to go in and turn off the alarm."

"Sure." Once again I had second thoughts about being here, but reasoned Deacon wouldn't have given me keys if he hadn't meant for me to stay here.

What I wasn't prepared for was how emotional it would be stepping through this door as if I was reliving our weekend together by being in his space. Dammit. It even smelled like him.

Maybe this wasn't the best idea after all. But as I was about to type in the security code, I realized the alarm wasn't set.

The sound of acoustic guitar chords suddenly started. Soft and steady, I followed the notes into the living room, finding none other than Deacon sitting on his couch strumming his guitar.

He stopped and looked up at me with a sexy smile. "Hi, Andi."

"You're here." And he hadn't told me he was in town.

He stood up, putting his guitar to the side, looking sexy and calm. "I am."

"I didn't know. I'd only meant to use the house a few days, but I'll go."

"Andi, no, I knew you'd be here I came here for you."

"You did?"

"Yes. I was going to tell you, but then you texted you were coming to the house, so I thought to surprise you."

He ran a hand through his hair, and I noticed the bags under his eyes for the first time.

"Are you all right?"

"Not really? Do you know why?"

I shook my head slowly while he framed my face with his hands. Hands I'd missed touching my skin.

"Not even an hour into the flight I wished I'd invited you with me."

My eyes went wide. "But you made it clear you didn't want me there."

He stepped back, but took my hand. "I know and I'm sorry. I wasn't prepared for this." He motioned between us. "I've never wanted someone in my space before."

I hadn't allowed myself to hope he might want more than our one weekend together. "What about your songwriting?"

"I had total writer's block for the first time. My inability felt like a message letting me know I was missing you." His thumb stroked over my cheek. "I figured I'd stay in LA for as long as you need to be here, what with selling the house and all. But once you've taken care of all that and are ready, maybe you could come to my house in Australia. I could show you around there."

He wasn't done with his pitch. "You could bring Callie with you. And if you can only spend a few days, that's fine. We can fly back here whenever you want or need to. I know you have a lot going on." He blew out a nervous breath. "I just want a chance to get to know you better, you know, have you see my place, and take you out on a proper date."

Unlike my ex, Deacon didn't minimize what I had going on in my life or try to manipulate my decisions. He'd proven again and again that I could trust him. "Callie and I would love to join you in Australia."

He dropped his lips to mine. "I know this sounds crazy, but I don't care. I fucking missed you, Andi."

The way he said my nickname would never get old. "I missed you too. And this can't be any crazier than our first kiss happening in front of a crowd of thousands at a concert I almost didn't attend, or my pretending to be a couple for a weekend in order to deal with our crazy exes."

He flashed a lopsided smile. "Imagine time together that doesn't include thoughts about our exes or the idea of faking it."

I returned his smile, the thrill of spending time together for real starting to sink in. "What would we possibly do with all that extra time?"

"I have lots of ideas." He captured my lips in a searing kiss.

While his mouth migrated to my neck, I ran my hands through his hair. "As much as I love the direction your thoughts are obviously taking, Ollie is outside with Callie." I paused, realizing he'd been out there awhile. "Did he know you were here?"

His smile got sheepish. "I might've given him a heads-up I was coming back."

"How soon could we leave for Australia?"

He pulled back to lean his forehead against mine. "Say the word."

"My luggage is in the car, and my passport's in my purse, so is tomorrow too soon?"

He kissed the sensitive spot below my ear, murmuring, "My brave girl." Then he stepped away to grab his phone. "How about I schedule the trip while you invite Ollie inside?"

Later that night after Ollie had said his goodbyes, Deacon and I sat outside on his deck overlooking the city, a delivered pizza on the table between us along with a bottle of red wine.

He shook his head in a slow, sexy way. "This doesn't count as our first real date."

I took a sip from the glass he'd poured. "Do you know how I like my first dates?"

A smile tugged at his lips. "Tell me."

"I like my first dates with a taste of red wine, the smell of pizza, a gorgeous view, and your company."

His gaze locked on mine. Taking my free hand from across the table, he kissed the inside of my wrist. "This is the best date I've ever been on."

The sincerity in his voice left no doubt he meant it. Setting my glass down, I got up from my chair and moved to his lap, loving the way he set his own glass down and put his arms around me.

"Prepare yourself; it's about to get better."

He nuzzled his face into my neck, breathing deep. "It already is."

EPILOGUE

Andrea

*T*he first time I saw Deacon in concert, I'd been fresh off a breakup and hardly paying attention to the other fans or the performance until I got called up on stage.

This time, seven months later, I took in every detail from my front-row seat at a music festival in LA. I saw everything, from the way the crowd knew his songs, the first note on, to the way everyone danced along and shouted his name.

It felt strange to share the man I loved with the world, yet at the same time I felt so proud to see him in his element. And yeah, every time he met my gaze, I could feel the tingle clear down to my toes.

Would I ever get used to how this man gave me shivers? I'd only planned to spend a couple weeks in Australia, but that short stay had turned into months. And four months into that, Deacon had asked me to move in with him.

His oasis in Australia was incredible. The main building of the three pavilions in the compound boasted a gourmet kitchen and a spacious living space. The second building, my favorite, held the master suite with an incredible four-poster bed and an en-suite bathroom. A plunge pool right outside the door formed the foreground of the ocean view.

The third and final pavilion was his songwriting retreat with comfortable sofas and a state-of-the-art gym. It really was an oasis, and I never got tired of taking walks down the path to the beach or exploring the incredible wildlife Australia had to offer.

My house had sold with an all-cash offer, making it quick and painless. After the televised interview about my breakup and with the public interest in my relationship with Deacon, the network had offered me a sizable amount to return to *City of Angels.* I'd declined and had zero regrets.

At the concert, Deacon finished a song and started talking up the audience. "Hello, LA, it's so good to be back here. I'm about to drop a new album next month and thought I'd debut a song from it here today."

I assumed he'd start to play the first single off the album. Instead, he motioned to his stage manager, and a spotlight suddenly shone on me. I was stunned and barely registered his next words.

"Won't you welcome to the stage, my girlfriend, the beautiful Andrea Roberts?"

The crowd went nuts even though he hadn't used the name they all knew from *City of Angels*. The instant my divorce had been finalized two weeks ago, I'd shed myself of my ex-husband's surname and gone back to the one I'd grown up with.

Like the last time Deacon had done this to me, it took Ollie to snap me out of my trance. "Go on up there, lovely," he urged from the seat beside me.

Right. On shaky legs, I walked to the edge of the stage. There, I was assisted up the steps by security. Leave it to Deacon to stand there with a sexy smirk.

"You know, LA, Andrea and I had our very first kiss here in front of a crowd. So I thought it only fitting that she be up here on stage when I sing the song I wrote about her during the very first weekend we spent together."

Holy shit. Of course, I knew he'd written some words down months ago, but he hadn't once mentioned it since.

A chair was produced from somewhere, and one of the stagehands led me to it. Meanwhile the band started to strum the chords of an unfamiliar song.

"In the morning when the sun shines on her face,
I know she's in the right place.
My brave girl..."

I'd never believed in out-of-body experiences, but sitting there on stage listening to the man I loved serenade me in front of tens of thousands of people sent me straight into one.

I didn't realize I had tears streaming down my face until the song ended and Deacon pulled me up from my chair to wipe the moisture away with his thumbs. His expression was pure concern until I finally smiled and threw my arms around his neck.

"It was so beautiful," I whispered, still not convinced this wasn't a dream.

His lips found mine and the deafening sound of the crowd faded away. Just like the first time he'd kissed me, the magic was still there. But this time he topped it.

"I love you, Andi."

"I love you too. So much."

With one last kiss, he flipped on the mic again. "Let's hear it for my brave girl, LA."

The fans went nuts, and I was sure my face was bright red as I walked off to the side of the stage where Deacon's manager greeted me.

DEACON

I closed out the festival with my last six songs, my biggest hits, and said goodnight to Los Angeles.

I'd expected Andrea to get emotional about me singing "Brave Girl" to her, but I hadn't anticipated how emotional it would make me to see her there on stage listening to every word.

She was the love of my life. I truly believed that every day I spent with her. And although I'd contemplated getting down on one knee in front of the world to ask her to spend the rest of her life with me, I decided that question would be something I'd ask in private.

Bounding off of the stage, I greeted her with a hug that took her off her feet. "Have I told you you're the best thing to ever happen to me?" I whispered in her ear, hard-pressed to let her go.

While it was true that she looked incredible in the little black dress she was wearing tonight, something that showed off the curves I adored, that wasn't what had me overwhelmed. During the entire concert, she'd sung along to my songs as if she was so proud to be there with me. This was something I hadn't even known I'd needed.

She grinned. "You haven't told me that before today, but you did write and perform a song about me, so I guess I'll let it slide."

My grin matched hers. For years, I'd had a team around to help make me successful. But aside from my mother, I'd never felt like I had someone who loved me for who I was. Someone who cared about me outside of the fame. I felt as though I could walk away from this lifestyle tomorrow, and she'd still love me just as much. It was such a powerful feeling.

"Come on. Our families are waiting."

My mom, stepfather, and stepbrother, along with Ollie and his partner, were all waiting outside in the shuttle van which was taking us to dinner. Although I was sorry to hear Bryce was going through a divorce from Nina, I'd be lying to say I wasn't relieved to have her out of all of our lives. The last I'd heard, he was dating again, and I hoped he too could find someone special.

At our table in a private room of a local seafood restaurant, we sat there with the laughter and wine flowing, Andrea's hand in mine. Although I loved living with her in Australia in our bubble, I also recognized how important our family and friends were. That's why we'd visited her parents before coming here. Although they'd been wary about meeting me, by the end of the three days, we were in a comfortable place. Especially after I'd gone fishing with her father.

The burning issue on my mind was when and where to pop the question. Logic told me to wait longer than the couple weeks following the finalization of her divorce, but frankly, we'd never measured our relationship according to time or what might have made sense to others.

My plan was to wait and do something romantic. Perhaps I could ask her while we were on the beach. Or maybe I could plan something special on our one-year anniversary.

But later that night as she lay naked in my arms, her trusted companion, Callie, in her bed at the foot of ours, I found myself unable to wait a moment longer.

"Marry me."

She sat up in bed suddenly. "Wh-what?"

I sat up with her. "For weeks I've been trying to think of

how and when to ask, but it turns out I can't wait a minute longer." Slipping out of the bed, I reached into the nightstand drawer to retrieve the velvet box I'd received yesterday from a local jeweler.

I scrambled for my PJ bottoms and tried to pull them on with my free hand. "Sorry, I didn't mean to propose naked."

She giggled when I nearly toppled over while wrestling with my clothing. "Oh, I don't know, I kind of think you being naked ups your chances."

I didn't blush easily, but leave it to Andi to make me do so. After finally winning the battle to put on some pants, I dropped to one knee.

"Convincing you to spend a weekend in LA with me was the absolute best decision I've ever made. But one weekend together wasn't nearly enough. And now I want them all. Will you do me the honor of becoming my wife?"

She launched herself at me. "Yes. A big fat yes."

Taking the vintage five-carat diamond out of the box, I slipped it on her ring finger. Then I stood up and pulled her next to me so I could kiss her. Sliding my hands down here bare back, I quipped, "Maybe naked proposals are the way to go."

She leaned back, grinning. "I'm a fan."

"I don't want to pressure you to pick a date, and we can wait as long as you want…" I wanted to be sensitive to her wishes even though I was anxious to move on with our future. "But I was thinking about just you and me on the beach and a party with our families sometime later. But if you want them there for the ceremony, then we could do something different." A big wedding with lots of guests wasn't my idea of the ideal wedding, but I didn't want to short her the dream if that's what she wanted.

She put her hands on either side of my face. "I'd marry

you tomorrow on the beach, or anywhere else for that matter. Because my life, the real one I was meant to live and be happy in, started the moment I met you."

Jesus. I swallowed past the lump in my throat. I don't know what I'd done to deserve this beautiful woman, but I'd do everything I could in life to give her the world. I could picture her as the mother to our children and raising a family together. The thought alone made me emotional.

I kissed her lips softly. "I cannot wait to marry you."

She threw her arms around my neck. "I can't wait to marry you too."

"What do you say, Andi? Wanna make some plans for the weekend?"

Her lips turned up in a grin that matched mine. "My favorite question ever."

Want another book set in LA? Be sure to check out Miss Understanding, an enemies to lovers, boss, assistant romance!

ACKNOWLEDGMENTS

A big thank you to Lissanne Jones for sharing her idea of a collection of "One Weekend In" books taking place in various cities throughout the world and asking me to be a part of it. It was only fitting we'd chat about it while in LA.

Thank you to my editor, Alyssa Kress for always making my books better! And to Judy Zweifel for her proofreading eagle eyes.

Sending mad love to my ARC team, and to all of my readers who pick up my books and love the characters like I do! You keep me motivated to write more stories!

Printed in Great Britain
by Amazon